AF244472

Driftwood

Driftwood

Harper Fox

Dedicated to Josh Lanyon, a mentor and friend
whose endless patience, generosity and inspiration
gave this story its wings

FoxTales Publications
www.harperfox.net

Driftwood
Copyright © 2017 by Harper Fox
ISBN 978-1-910224-21-2

Cover art by Harper Fox
Image licensed through Shutterstock
All rights reserved

This is a work of fiction. Any resemblance to persons living or dead is entirely coincidental.

Chapter One
The Seventh Wave

Thomas walked slowly on the edge of the world, to discover what the sea would bring him.

He seldom took anything home, unless it was a stone or piece of driftwood Belle had particularly set her heart on. There was no space for clutter in his spartan rooms, and his tastes did not incline towards collecting. But sometimes there were things to look at and put back—fantastic conch shells, pieces of the green rock called serpentine that washed in from the Kynance cliffs to the southeast. If he found a piece of round white quartz, he might take that, and later add it to the pile outside his door that he tried hard not to think of as a cairn.

The morning was cold, the bay wreathed in sea fret. Fairly typical for late April on this lonely Cornish coast, and Thomas found the chill perversely comforting. He didn't mind the tourist season, but would miss his solitary walks out here along the sea's edge. In a couple of weeks' time there would be vehicles other than his own battered Land Rover pulled up in the little beach car park, the first hopeful surfers of the season piling out onto the tarmac in a welter of boards, wetsuits and towels. They were mostly peaceful souls, pilgrims seeking out the magic of this wild coast, and God knew their tourist spending kept the local economy afloat.

Thomas blinked and came to a halt on the wet sand. There was one of them out there already. He pushed his mist-dampened fringe out of his eyes and looked again. The sharp onshore wind was heaping the surf into short-lived grey mountains, surely too turbulent for even the craziest of riders. He frowned and sensed Belle coming to stand beside him, the top of her elegant wolfhound head pressing lightly to his elbow. No. He couldn't see anyone now. It had been a momentary impression, of a lean silver shape poised between one wave crest and the next. A shudder rolled through him. It wouldn't be his first hallucination, but he'd hoped very much that he had seen his last. His fingers sought the rough silk of Belle's scruff, unconsciously reaching for solidity, warmth. "Come on, dog. Let's go home."

He turned to leave, but Belle remained fixed to the spot. When he called to her again, she whined. Thomas turned in surprise. It was a lonely sound, poignant in the mist, and he had seldom heard it. The people at the shelter had said she scarcely ever vocalised, which had been one of his reasons for choosing her as a companion, despite her vast size and matching appetite. He went back to her, and the sound came again, like a foghorn heard from far out at sea. She was rigid, poised, looking back towards the waves.

Thomas followed the direction of her gaze and saw it too. Not a hallucination, then, unless the dog was sharing it. A ghost, maybe. This haunted coast had plenty of stories. A Flying Dutchman surfer, plying the Atlantic storm in endless solitude. Probably enough of them had died out there by now to spawn a few ghosts.

As Thomas watched, the graceful figure, still little more than a shadow in the mist, caught a perfect wave and began his ride. He was a long way out, but seemed to spot the watchers on the shore and lifted one hand in an insouciant salute.

No ghost would be so bloody stupid. Thomas turned away in disgust. Since returning from his third and final tour of duty as an army medical officer, he had struggled to hold together the bodies and souls that fell under his care as village doctor in his native Sankerris. Usually it was nothing worse than sprained muscles and arthritis, but even in peaceful West Cornwall, drug-addiction cases came his way, cancers, sick children. And as for the years before that, Thomas kept his thoughts about the sand and bloodstained dust, his efforts to mend shattered soldiers in the Camp Bastion field hospital, in a well-sealed box. He had no time for lunatics who took their lives in their hands for no better reason than to chase a thrill.

The mystique and beauty of the surfing community's ideals were not lost on him, but most were content to wait for decent weather and the seasonal lifeguards who would start work a couple of weeks into May. They did not go out alone, in waves big enough to swallow a house, doubtlessly expecting coastguards and air-sea rescue men to risk their lives in turn to fish them out when the inevitable happened. Realising that the dull, slow swell of rage inside him was little to do with this one dumb kid on a board and a lot to do with the post-traumatic stress disorder he could simultaneously diagnose in himself and utterly deny, that it was eight o'clock in the morning and he had patients who deserved a better doctor than the one he would turn into if he didn't get a grip on himself, Thomas lowered his head and began to stride back up the beach.

Belle howled. It was once only, but Thomas's blood ran cold. The sound bounced off the granite cliffs behind him, seemed to blend itself with the roar of the surf, as if the sea had found a voice. Insofar as Thomas was still capable of affection, he loved the dog. Seized by a fear he couldn't name, he ran back to her. "Belle, you silly bitch. What's the matter?" Belle ignored him, and Thomas once more followed the cue of her unfathomable amber-eyed stare.

Just in time to see the surfer execute a sublime passage through the barrel of a breaker, hit the deadly Porth Bay rip, and take the most devastating wipeout Thomas had seen in thirty years of watching riders fly and crash along this coast. For a moment he was lost in admiration. The move had been so beautiful, its termination so complete, that it was almost satisfying, answered some marrow-deep impulse to destruction inside him. He waited, calculating the speed and direction of the rip, adding in a few yards for the undertow. He could work out, more or less, where this talented lunatic should surface.

It didn't happen. Thomas swallowed hard. This was none of his business. He had come out to walk his dog, just as he did every morning, same time, same place, part of a rigid routine whose component parts could be fitted together, end to end, to form a normal day. The lunatic would be fine. Anyone who could surf like that could surely swim with equal power. He would survive, even if the wave whose belly he had threaded was still in the process of breaking, a mountain of water thundering down, rolling and roiling into its own roots. Thomas knew how that felt. No surfer himself, he had once loved the sea, and you didn't grow up around here without learning the force of those green-grey Atlantic monsters that swelled in, heaped themselves up on the continental shelf, and expended their momentum with bruising, crushing vigour on human limbs. It was seldom fatal. There was an exhilaration in being caught up in them, like surviving a benign rockfall. If you could swim, if you knew the rip pattern, you generally lived.

Thomas shielded his eyes with one hand. The board would pop up first, dragging its owner to surface by the ankle. None of his business at all.

First, do no harm. Thomas, about to walk away, shivered to a halt. Eight bitter years since he had taken his Hippocratic oath, and he was certain he had violated it in a dozen ways. The war his nation was waging in the far-off desert he had left behind to come home and fit himself into the shape of the man he once had been—that formless, limitless, probably endless fucking war—it hadn't been conducive to good and dignified medical practice. Hippocrates probably had not foreseen the necessity of punching a wounded soldier unconscious to silence his raging objection to the failed Afghani suicide bomber being treated in the next bed. Of taking a rifle from a corpse and sniping off a bunch of gun-toting local kids across a wall of sandbags to defend the bleeding and helpless survivors at his feet. *First, do no harm...* It made Thomas want to laugh, or throw up, but he knew that to turn his back on the ocean now would be a harm his own fragmented soul might not survive. He felt inside his jacket for his mobile.

Which, for once, was not safely tucked inside its purpose-tailored pocket. Thomas swore. He always carried it. Joggers came out here, overdid it and keeled over with heart attacks all the time. Kids wandered; old ladies fell down steps. Something might happen to Belle. Unforgivably, this morning he had left it in the Rover, down between the seats where it had landed when he'd swerved to avoid a badger. It seemed this morning no one was taking care. By the time he ran up the half mile or so to the car park...

Frantically he scanned the beach, but he'd chosen his wilderness well, and there was no one to be seen in either direction.

He undid the jacket and let it drop onto the sand. He hadn't been in the ocean for years, but his army service had left him fit and hard. He could feel the neglected strength inside himself, waiting. He kicked off his shoes. That would have to do. He swam, as routinely and rigidly as he did everything else, three times a week at the pool in Penzance. Taking one last guess at where that stupendous, still-breaking wave might have deposited the surfer—or, by now, his corpse—Thomas ran into the sea.

The stinging cold hit him instantly, emptying his lungs. You forgot, between visits. Forgot the riptide, tearing at your legs even knee-high, forgot the high pure chill, like a cry, a long, beautiful, unbearable note of music that would not end. The Gulf Stream was slowing, Thomas had heard. He could believe it. The water surged up his thighs, forcing a yelp from him as it engulfed his cock and testicles, none of which equipment, he imagined, would ever be seen again. He took a few more strides and got ready for the plunge.

Something knocked his legs from under him. The impact was hard, warm, human-sized. Crashing down into the surf, Thomas grabbed instinctively at the object—surfer, dolphin, at very worst juvenile shark—which had mown him down. Held it, anchoring it and himself against the immediate seize of the undertow. An unequal battle—the monster wave, having spent itself, was now sucking back down the steeply pitching shore, creating a drag like steel cables. Thomas had to get his feet beneath him or he and whatever piece of flotsam he was clutching would be hauled straight back out. But the sand beneath his scrabbling fingers was shaly and lacking cohesion, grains and pebbles sliding off each other in the salty churn.

A tug at the back of his neck, then a sharp, tearing pain. Thomas cried out in atavistic fear. The body he was clutching to him in one arm was encased in rubber, not the astounding natural vinyl of shark skin, but nonetheless something had just closed its teeth in his shoulder. The pull it exerted and the panic it sent through his limbs enabled him to get his head above the crashing surf, find his centre of gravity and lurch upright.

Belle stood planted a yard or so behind him, soaked and mute. She looked as if she would have liked to speak to him, but the three-inch scrap of his shirt fabric hanging from her mouth was eloquent enough. Thomas coughed, shook water from his eyes. "Jesus, Belle."

The deadweight he was holding by its armpits suddenly came to life. Staggering, fighting not to go down in the thigh-high rip, Thomas aided its struggle to flip over and get to its feet. For a long moment they stared at one another. Thomas had time to be surprised. He had been expecting some kid, a salt-bleached surf freak with a shark's-tooth necklace who'd seen *Point Break* one too many times. The man in front of him, grazed and blue-lipped but now propping Thomas against the current in his turn, looked only a couple of years younger than himself. He was lean and dynamically built, radiating heat through the pro-quality wetsuit under Thomas's hands. His hair was plastered down, its colour indeterminate, but there was no doubt about his eyes, green as the sea which had just thrown him back out of her maw, fixed on Thomas's, full of laughter and contrition. He said, "Christ, I'm sorry. Thank you."

Then he glanced over his shoulder, back towards the water, out of which a rushing sound was coming, a wild roar that somehow neither of them had noticed. "Run!"

The only thing bigger than the seventh wave is the ninth wave that follows it—another piece of ocean lore Thomas had absorbed during his boyhood and for some reason briefly forgotten. The surfer gave him only an instant to look back, long enough to see that the overcast morning sky had turned to foam-streaked glass. *A ninth one, gathering half the deep…and all the wave was in a flame,* soared up from Thomas's memory, lines learned and loved long ago, forgotten also, and then the surfer's hand closed on his own, a hot, tight grip he would remember.

They made it about eight yards inshore, not far, but crucial. When the wave hit, it knocked them down and forward, into water too shallow for the undertow to seize them again. It was still like being caught in an avalanche, a bloody cosmic washing machine, tumbling them limb over limb into a coughing, spitting heap in the shale. When finally it receded, Thomas found to his bewilderment that the breath he'd managed to snatch wanted to leave him in laughter. Then rage bloomed, dark and satisfactory, sweet as arousal. He couldn't remember the last time he'd given vent to it. He tore himself out of the grip of the surfer, who was trying to help him to his feet, and gave him a shove that sent him down onto his expensively Neoprene-clad backside once more. "You bloody moron!"

Belle, who had never heard him raise his voice any more than he had heard her raise hers, came trotting down from her safe refuge higher up the sand and took up an anxious position at his side.

"You stupid fuck!" Salt water rose up and choked him, briefly checking his momentum. "Do you think I care about you? What about the poor bastards who have to come and get you? You think you're worth a helicopter, a lifeboat—all those lives?"

The surfer gazed up at him. His eyelashes were matted together with salt, the grazing to his brow and cheekbone beginning to bleed copiously. He didn't look resentful at the tirade—waited patiently till his rescuer had run out of breath and was coughing again, hands propped on his knees. "The RNLI boys know not to come out for me. One of the Hawke Lake choppers is out of commission, and the other two are off to Devon for the air show. That's why I chose today."

"What?"

"That's why I chose today to surf."

"No. I… How do you know all that? And how do you come to have an arrangement with the Royal National bloody Lifeboat Institute?"

The surfer smiled. "Lieutenant Flynn Summers," he offered, holding out a hand. "Search-and-rescue unit, Royal Naval Air Service. At your disposal."

Thomas straightened up. He was calm now. He steadied himself with one hand on Belle's collar, and surveyed his new acquaintance, outstretched hand and all, with dispassion. He said flatly, "Of all the people who should bloody well know better," and walked off.

His cold detachment carried him a good twenty yards or so. He wished he could do better, keep his head down and march off in good earnest, leaving this flotsam to fend for itself. He was not sure what was stopping him. Why, at the edge of the dunes, he found himself slowing down.

The wind had shifted. If Summers had needed him, had called out to him for help, Thomas wouldn't have heard. He was aware that, for all the display of bravado, the fool had come within a hairsbreadth of drowning. Beneath his wetsuit, he had to be bruised down to the bone. Why would a rescue pilot, a military one at that, put himself through such a wipeout? No one could have ridden the surf here today. He must have known he would crash and had carried on regardless. What had he been looking for? Peace? Release? There had been a fever in his gaze. *Expiation*, Thomas thought suddenly, though for what crimes he couldn't possibly imagine. He stopped, and reluctantly turned and looked back.

He needn't have worried. Summers was on his feet and jogging down the beach away from him. As Thomas watched, he came to a halt and scooped up a bundle of clothes Thomas only at that point recognised were his own discarded jacket and boots.

For God's sake. He would have to try harder not to get angry. It stripped from him any frail dignity he had been managing to accrue for himself. He'd been ready to stalk off barefoot from this encounter. He supposed he might have noticed when he reached the gravelled car park.

Anger made him bloody uncivil too. Dismissive and unjust. He was—or had been—too good a combat-zone medic to judge a patient's book by its cover, especially when it came to soldiers. He had seen Lieutenant Summers' brand of panache before, in men too proud or shaken to admit that they were hurt. Having gathered up Thomas's things, he was now jogging after him, or trying to. He wasn't steady on his feet. Thomas saw that his left ankle was grazed raw where the tough Velcro cuff of his surfboard had torn off him. He managed three or four strides, then crashed to hands and knees in the sand.

Thomas ran to him. He unfolded him gently from his cramped-up curl, made him sit with his head down while he picked up his jacket. Summers shuddered as the warm, fragrant leather descended round his shoulders, then again as Thomas briefly brushed a palm across his skull.

"You'll be all right." The tone came easy to him. Detached but kind. He'd said it to boys who were breathing their last in his arms, and watched the fear leave their eyes as they believed him. "You've just had a bit of a knock. Sit there for a minute. Then come back to my car. I've got some coffee, and I'll run you in to Penzance casualty for a check."

Summers raised his head. "I'm okay. I'll take the coffee, but I really don't expect anybody to—"

"That's right," Thomas interrupted him, dryly but without irritation. Now that he had this man tagged in his mind as a patient, not some wild-card rogue with the power to disrupt his day, to get life and death out of the separate boxes to which he had assigned them and tangle them up around his feet, he could be kind. "Because when the lifeboat crew hear someone's in trouble, they're gonna say, *oh, it's just that idiot from the air base, let's not bother.* Aren't they?"

Summers sat quietly, clearly absorbing a new point of view. He did not look to Thomas like a man who submitted easily. Thomas found himself puzzled and oddly touched. Summers was even beginning a faint blush—of shame? Then he frowned at Thomas distractedly and said, "You're bleeding."

Thomas almost laughed. That was rich, coming from someone who now looked like he'd just survived a shark attack. Head wounds bled profusely anyway, and the salt water was making it worse. His shoulder was stinging, though, and he touched the rip in his shirt. "Yeah. My own damn dog bit me."

He helped Summers up and let him take a few uncertain steps on his own before reaching to support him. It was only a hand to his elbow, but Summers flinched as if the contact burned him.

"Are you all right?" Thomas enquired, loosening his grasp. "Does your arm hurt?"

"No. Well—yes, it does, but not there." He shook his head. "Sorry. I'm freaked out a bit. I don't know why."

"Shock, probably." Thomas kept his voice level. He was freaked out too, but he had no easy explanation for his own state, or why it was hard for him to make the ordinary doctorly gesture of helping this young man off the beach. "Here. Can you put your arm round my shoulders?"

"Yeah. Thanks. Er... I'll have to give you your jacket back first." Summers slipped it off his shoulders and handed it to Thomas, making a rueful face at the patterns drying sea salt was making on the leather. "Shit. I'll have that dry-cleaned for you."

"What? Oh, no. Belle does worse than that to it when she's been in the mud." Thomas shrugged into the jacket, unwillingly aware that it would be easier to have Summers' arm around him, Summers' warm flank pressed to his side, if there were a shielding layer in place between them, not just his own wet shirt. Why, for God's sake? Why were Thomas's nerves singing, prickles of gooseflesh trying to lift up the hairs on his nape? Handsome Lieutenant Summers probably had an equally presentable girlfriend waiting for him at home, if not a young wife and a couple of blossoming kids. And even if he were queer as fuck, what difference should that make to Thomas? All that was over for him, long dead and buried in the Afghan dust. Shaking himself, he reached out an arm to Summers, who was hanging back, looking at least as uneasy as Thomas felt. "Come here. It's okay."

They set off together up the beach. Thomas soon realised that the jacket wasn't providing much defence against sensation. Every step brought Summers into light, insistent contact against him. Too damn light—Summers, understandably wary, was stiff and awkward in his embrace. His arm round Thomas was an obedient gesture only, exerting no weight. And he needed the support. His breath was coming shallowly and too fast.

Thomas took hold of the wrist draped over his shoulder, silently reproaching himself once more for his outburst. "Lean on me," he said, and felt Summers relax a little.

Better and worse. Conflicting desires tore at Thomas. He was helping Summers properly now, justifying their proximity with his strength and his medical purpose. They would cover the couple of hundred yards between here and the car park in no time. Thomas wouldn't have to cope for long with this sweet, profoundly unsettling pressure at his side.

And, perversely, he minded. The distance was suddenly too long and too damn short all at once. He needed and wanted and could hardly bear the thought of letting go. He frowned, bewildered at himself, struggling for control. Here at last were the beginnings of the long ramp that led up to the promenade. Summers winced as they negotiated the stones and bits of concrete half hidden in the sand, and Thomas concentrated fiercely on keeping him upright.

He tugged open the Land Rover's rear door and released Summers carefully to sit on her rusty step. The car park was still deserted, though the sun had boiled off the last of the sea fret and the first really fine day of the season was promising in the periwinkle sky over the cliffs. Reaching awkwardly past him, Thomas extracted a thermos of coffee from under the back seat. As well as a good deal of glass-enhanced warmth, the Rover's interior was exuding pleasant if basic scents: leather, vinyl, clean dog. Summers leaned back into the heat, shivering, and Thomas quickly poured him a cup of coffee from the flask. "Here you are."

"Thanks." Summers accepted it gratefully, lifting the cup to blue-tinged lips. "Oh, that's nice."

Thomas smiled. Habitually he made himself up a batch of Kenyan from the cafetière. He hadn't been expecting to share it. He was peripherally glad that it was decent—perhaps it offset the fact that the four-by-four looked ready to crumble to scrap where it stood. Thomas seldom noticed the state of his vehicle, but something in the action of helping Summers across the car park towards it had made him aware of its shortcomings. "Good. Drink it slowly. Do you feel sick or disoriented?"

"Er… No. I don't think so."

"Okay. Move over a bit." Thomas leaned past him again, this time extracting a tartan car rug and his first-aid kit. He handed Summers the rug. "Here. Put that round you." Setting the box down on the tarmac, he crouched beside it and flipped up the lid. "Not sleepy?"

"No. Not irritable, either, and I reckon my pulse and BP are fine."

Thomas glanced up. Summers, of course, would know the signs of immersion hypothermia as well as he did. Better, probably. "Okay," he said wryly. "Good."

"I know you, don't I?" Summers asked. "You're the village doctor up at Sankerris."

Thomas, busy tearing open an antiseptic pad, frowned in surprise. He didn't get many flyboys through his surgery, the RNAS base having state-of-the-art facilities, though sometimes when they started families they preferred to bring their children to him. "That's right. Thomas Penrose. Have we met?"

"No. I drive through Sankerris on my way to the base sometimes, and I've noticed you, that's all."

Thomas saw him start to blush, and looked away to let him off the hook. He was ridiculously disconcerted himself, at the idea of having been noticed—by another man, or this one, anyway, explicitly and unavoidably gorgeous in his Neoprene skin. Thomas made no efforts to be seen. He knew that he was still in decent shape, but he dressed quietly, kept his profile low. Other than that—well, the man who stared back at him from mirrors these days was almost a stranger. Brown eyes, once expressive, now guarded, always looking to a dangerous horizon. Thomas kept this stranger tidy, made sure its dark hair never grew out of its soldierly crop. He was not noticeable.

"Oh, right," he said vaguely, and reached up with the antiseptic pad. "Sorry. This is gonna sting a bit."

Summers sat patiently while Thomas cleaned sand out of the grazing on his face and neck. Thomas, who usually had no trouble with an impersonal touch—it was the other kind that fazed him these days—found that he was having to concentrate hard on his work. This man's proximity troubled him. To push his wet hair back from his brow was disquieting, made Thomas want simultaneously to do it again and to flinch away. Biting his lip, he finished out his task, steeling himself to non-reaction when Summers tilted his head to one side to accommodate the clean-up, exposing delicate tendons in his throat.

"Thanks," Summers said, when it was done. "Now, give me that and hold still for a minute."

Thomas found himself obeying. Now that Summers' face was clear of blood, his hair beginning to dry tawny blond in the sun, he looked younger, maybe only in his mid-twenties. But there was a compelling note in his voice, a shade of authority, and Thomas supposed you did not get to a lieutenant's rank in the Navy without some powers of command.

Oh God. To be tended was almost unbearable. This was not the dynamic of Thomas's world—*he* was the healer. He saw to others. No one looked after him. On the rare occasions of his own illness or injury, he dealt with it himself. Summers' fingers on his skin sent ripples of shock through him, although the other man was only gently easing back the collar of his shirt to examine the place where Belle's teeth had grazed him. Clenching his hands on the Land Rover's step, Thomas stared grimly at the tarmac while Summers sloshed antiseptic over the wound then pressed the pad to it tight.

"There," he said. "I don't think it needs stitching, but look out for infection. You know, dog bites... To be fair to her, though, I think she was trying to help you."

"I know." Thomas drew a deep breath and managed not to flinch out from under Summers' hands as he pulled a wide strip of plaster from the kit and smoothed it into place on his shoulder. "She's a good girl."

Raising his head, he was about to wonder where she was—then saw her, regally seated by Summers' side. He hadn't seen her jump in. He found he was mildly chagrined. Belle was almost as mistrustful of strangers as himself, another reason, along with her good manners, why he had chosen her. Now she was looking down her long grizzled nose at Summers, in evident approval. A little silence fell. It was not awkward, stitched through as were most Land's End silences with seagull cries and wave song, but Thomas felt a strain on his nerves. It had been a long time since he had spoken properly to someone who was not a patient, and longer than he could remember since he had been touched.

Flynn Summers was smiling at him. Distantly, reluctantly, Thomas noted his beauty, like a half-remembered echo from another world. "Well," he said hoarsely. "If you're really okay..."

Summers got stiffly to his feet. "Yes." He shook the sand out of the rug, folded it and handed it back. "I mustn't take up more of your time. Thank you, Dr. Penrose."

Thomas considered letting him hold on to the formality. He felt, unreasonably, that he needed the distance. But that would leave him stuck with *Lieutenant Summers*, and he'd given and received enough military titles to last him a lifetime. He put out a hand, remembering with shame that he hadn't been gracious enough to accept the other man's gesture before. "It's Thomas."

"Flynn. And I'll bear in mind what you said, about risking other people's lives."

"Oh." Detaching his hand from the strong grip enclosing it, Thomas flickered him an uneasy smile. "I tore your head off, didn't I? Sorry. I was going to say, if you're all right, can I give you a lift back to your car? Where are you parked?"

"No need. I'm just round the back of the café." Summers looked at him thoughtfully for a moment, then smiled, and said suddenly, startling them both a little, "Penrose, eh? Proper Cornish."

Thomas smiled too, for the first time broadly. "Born and bred. You?"

Before Flynn could answer, pattering footsteps on the seafront pavement beyond the car park made both of them look up. A plump, pink-faced woman in her late forties was jogging up the slope towards them, progress impeded by oversized carpet slippers. "Thomas!" she cried, waving frantically. "Oh, Tom. I thought I saw your car. *Please* will you come and talk to Victor? He's been in that damn boathouse for three days. He won't come out." Halting a few yards away, she looked the doctor up and down, her broad, kind face folding up in concern. "Oh my God, Tom. Has there been an accident?"

"Er… No. At least…we're all right. I'll come straight down." He turned to Flynn. "Sorry. I have to go."

"Course. Is there anything I can do?"

Thomas surveyed him. Flynn looked subtly different, for all he was still damp and bleeding. Thomas wondered if this was his professional mask, the one his rescued fishermen and capsized tourists saw. He was impressed with how thoroughly he had assumed it, erasing all trace of the slightly gauche young man who had just needed rescue himself. Ready for action. Just for an instant, Thomas let himself imagine how it would be to avail himself of the offer. Flynn looked solid, capable. What would it be like, not to have to go in and face poor Victor alone?

But Victor was wreckage from Thomas's own old war, not Flynn's. And all of Thomas's actions since his return had tended to his own isolation—he wanted, needed, had to be alone.

"No," he said, almost sharply. "I mean, no thank you. Just take care of yourself."

Briskly he turned and closed up the Land Rover, making sure a window was cracked down for Belle. He helped Flynn lift his board. It was a pro's eight-footer, and not a lightweight. They were always much heavier than they looked on the water, being used for purposes of flight by talented, graceful, intriguing lunatics like… He was suddenly acutely aware that, when he turned his back to follow Victor's wife down the street, that would be the last he would ever see of Flynn Summers. There was no reason to suppose otherwise. He felt a strange pang, almost like homesickness, a kind of resonant ache beneath his breastbone. And Flynn was watching him intently, as if he too had something more he wished to say.

But he only nodded, and lifted a hand, and set off barefoot across the car park. Thomas looked back—once, helplessly, as Florence seized his hand, and then again a minute later while she was tapping anxiously on the boathouse doors. The second time he saw Flynn up near the top of the pitching Porth Bay high street, thumb out to flag down a ride. The first few vehicles went past him. He'd be lucky, Thomas thought, wondering why he'd lied about having his car with him, wondering how he'd got down here in the first place. He needed a ride big enough to take him and the surfboard too. Then air brakes hissed, and a truck with RNAS livery pulled up beside him, and he was gone.

Chapter Two
Sea Glass

By the time he finished work that night, Thomas could think only of the watchtower and the uninterrupted silences that awaited him there. He got into the battered Land Rover and drove, up into the hills to the north of Sankerris, higher and higher through the narrow single tracks. Like most West Countrymen born, he could drive as adroitly backwards as forwards, but this time met no oncoming tractors or tourists and was glad of it. It could be a matter of reversing a mile or more down the spiralling lanes, whose banks were beginning to heap up with wildflowers at this turn of the season. He just wanted to get home. He broached the horizon, where farmland flattened out to moor, and the north coast of the peninsula spread itself out for him, bare, wild and clean. Rolling the Rover's window down, he drew a deep breath of the sweet air.

There was the quoit. This was one of Thomas's commuting runs and he saw it every day, often twice, but it never failed to seize him. Placed here by unknown hands five thousand years before, knocked down in a storm and badly reconstructed in the 1800s, it was a stupendous thing, as breathtaking today as it must have been when its Neolithic builders had somehow raised its ten-ton flying capstone onto its four granite supports—three, now, after its clumsy rebuild—and set it to dominate the Morvah moor. West Penwith natives were blasé about it, calling it the tourist's quoit—set a bare hundred yards back from the road, it was easily visible for miles and, unlike most of the county's megalithic attractions, did not require a hike through gorse-tangled moorland to get to. For Thomas, the accessibility never diminished its magic. He was not even sure, on his daily drives past it, that it always lifted into view at the same place on his horizon, an effect he would put down to his own weariness.

Which, today, was extreme. Belle, who had lapsed into silence again, only changed the angle of her ears as they bypassed the quoit, but Thomas could read her disappointment. They often stopped here for a walk, and she'd had a long day of it, patiently waiting out his shift in the back room of the pharmacy. "Sorry, sweetheart. Not today." He saw her resume her queenly position in the passenger seat, watching the road ahead.

He drove until the Atlantic appeared, silver-glitter indigo, beyond the north coast's pitching cliffs, then took an unmarked side track and bounced the Rover across half a mile of moorland, the track fading out to turf and scattered stones beneath her tyres. He opened a farm gate, drove through and shut it behind him, then let Belle out of the passenger side. Restrained and polite, she seldom indulged in undignified racing around, but she did love her run home, and Thomas liked the sight, her full-power streak across the last tract of moor to the solitary white-painted building near the edge of the cliff.

He followed her in the Rover and pulled up outside the tower, ratcheting the handbrake up with a sigh of relief. By the time he had finished with poor Victor today, there'd been no time to come home for a change of clothes, and he'd had to start his surgery round as he was. Mrs. Vic had offered him a shirt, but none of her husband's mighty garments would have been less conspicuous on Thomas than his own wet ones, which by that time had started to dry on his skin. In his office, he resorted to his seldom-used white coat to hide the damage and had got away with it. Now, though, the cotton and denim, stiff with salt, were scraping on his skin, and he thought with longing of a shower. The bathroom was the only part of the watchtower he had bothered to have professionally refurbished—worth it, for a man who still hallucinated desert dust in the crevices of his body, whose dreams left his muscles so rigid with resistance he could often barely walk until he'd immersed himself in a bath.

The tower had its original black-oak door, the wood rock solid and satiny with time. Belle, still wild, was describing high-speed circles round the building, always clockwise, as if she shared the many local witches' aversion to a widdershins manoeuvre. Smiling, Thomas took the vast key from under its stone and began to let himself in.

He noticed the package at the same time the dog did, and both of them froze, Belle skidding to a halt on the turf. She trotted across to the door and sniffed the box over as if it had been an unexploded bomb, and Thomas reflected with a touch of shame that they were, after all, a pair of suspicious bastards. Then she sat down and looked up at him with an expression he could only interpret as a smile.

He carried the box into the house, wondering at its weight. He hadn't ordered anything. Placing it on the plain deal table in the kitchen, he noted from its labels that it had been sent up by parcel post from Marazion just that afternoon, and presumably at some expense—it was about eighteen inches all round and heavy as a rock. Thomas pulled out a kitchen chair, turned it round so he could straddle it and folded his arms along the back.

He wasn't in the mood for surprises. After seeing to poor Victor, he hadn't been in much of a mood for anything, except perhaps drinking himself to oblivion. That thought sparked another in his mind, one connected with the gleam of a rarely touched supply of vodka in a crate under the stairs. Breaking his own rules of seldom-on-weekdays and never-before-eight, Thomas dismounted from the chair and went to pour himself a generous double.

It was good, very smooth—his thinking had been that, if he spared no expense, he would go easy on it—but his throat was still raw with salt and unaccustomed shouting, and he choked faintly, pressing a hand to his mouth. What was in the damn box? He had an uneasy feeling in his gut about it. He was unsettled anyway. Having managed all day not to think about Flynn Summers, now that he was alone and unoccupied once more, he was finding he could think of little else. And people like Flynn did not belong in Thomas's life. He was no longer fit to associate with the young and the reckless, with men who were—Thomas felt it, even on shortest acquaintance—absolutely, essentially sweet-natured. Not innocent perhaps but not spoiled, not tainted as Thomas was.

No, Thomas's world was populated by the likes of Victor Travers, or their ghosts. Vic had served with him in Afghanistan. They had grown up together in Sankerris. Then Thomas had gone off to university, medical school, and Vic had stayed at home, apprenticed to his father's boat-building trade in the Porth Bay harbour. Thomas had next seen him at Bastion, a shell-shocked squaddie brought to him on a stretcher. Boredom had set in, Vic had explained to him, when he could talk. Boredom and lack of challenge. He had not needed to tell his old friend with what fervour he now wished himself back in the sweet, sleepy nowhere of the west. Thomas had patched him up and seen him sent back out.

And again. And again. When, after a leave of absence, Victor's sergeant called round to pick him up for the airbase and his third tour of duty, he found him in his dad's boathouse, staring blankly into space, his kit packed and ready, his service pistol held to his brow.

The sergeant had talked him out of that attempt, but there had been others, in the army psychiatric hospital and afterwards at home, where his distraught wife had tried to take care of him. Thomas, returning from his own third tour honourably discharged, had tried to help. He became Victor's GP, once the poor sod had worked through his allotted portion of army assistance and been turned loose on the world. He helped him with his compensation claim, a battle still ongoing as the government and upper military echelons conspired to prove that Gulf War syndrome and PTSD were only a specialised form of malingering, best cured by another spell on the front line.

Thomas supposed that if Vic had had his legs blown off in the service of his country, things might have been different. He helped him sign on for state incapacity benefit, persuading him that this was not an admission of weakness or failure. But what Victor needed from him most was his presence while he talked. Thomas had shared enough of his combat experiences to make him a good audience. Victor had lost all sense that his friend might reenact the dreadful scenes too, as he spoke, and not therapeutically. Once the kindest and most loving of men, Victor had come back from war clad in a brazen selfishness that made him blind to the pain of his wife, children, even a fellow soldier.

Thomas poured himself another drink, a treble this time. He had spent two hours in the boathouse this morning. By the time he had emerged into the light, Victor shambling at his side, he could scarcely feel the sun's warmth on his skin. He knew that it was there, but his capacity to feel it, to feel anything good, had been *unplugged*, was the closest term he could find. He felt unplugged, unhitched from his surroundings. On the rare but significant occasions when he drank, it was simply in order to make his body and brain match up. If he'd downed half a bottle of Stolichnaya Elit, he could expect to feel numb. It would be normal, and the next day he would have a normal hangover, recover and get back to work.

He reached for his glass. Before he could lift it, Belle came and laid her great long head upon the table beside it.

He hadn't fed her. Sighing, Thomas pushed to his feet. He knew what she was up to, of course. By the time he had shovelled out enough dog food to satisfy her, he would be more in need of a shower than ever, and would probably go and do that, leaving the drink on the table. The shower would clear his head, and when he came down he would see the thick file of paperwork Florence Travers had pushed into his hands before he left—the latest stage of Vic's appeal, to which Thomas was adducing medical evidence. It needed to be done tonight, and done sober.

He would write his letters and statements, maybe notice after that that he was hungry, maybe go and cook. These days he would live on ready meals happily enough, did not some distant sense that he was a doctor and should practise what he preached still prompt him to buy fresh meat and veg and prepare them in some vaguely becoming fashion.

Then he would wash up—everything, straightaway, the sight of dirty dishes and disorder making his stomach begin to twist in anxiety almost the second his meal was done. If he wanted to keep it down, he would do his chores. The rest of the house too. There wasn't much to it—one big round room on the ground floor, to which the kitchen was a recent extension, and a spiral of stairs that ran around the tower wall to another circular space, slightly smaller to allow for the taper of the building. Removing such traces of dust and untidiness as the rooms had accumulated during their long, silent, uninhabited day should not have taken long, but to do it to Thomas's standards—and he knew that he was sick, knew helplessly that this was not normal behaviour, and certainly not part of the man who had gone out to Afghanistan five years ago—required time, and huge amounts of energy. At some point during the process, he would become tired, as Belle knew. It would overwhelm him suddenly and utterly, and he would drop into sleep without any need of vodka to send him on his way.

Thomas looked at his dog. Her head was still on the table, her expression serene and unaltered. It didn't always work, God knew. Sometimes he just got wasted. But maybe not tonight.

***

The package was, of course, still there when he came down from his shower. Deciding to deal with the unknown factor before getting on with his evening's routine, Thomas sliced carefully through the parcel tape and plastic strips and lifted out from the first box a second one, neatly secured against impact by bubble wrap and polystyrene corners. This inner box was made of a thick, satiny cardboard, a kind of sea-green in colour, very beautiful. Its lid was impressed with a silver logo. Thomas suddenly recalled seeing boxes of this sort in the hands of visitors on the streets of Marazion, being reverently carried or cradled. *What the hell?* Gingerly he detached the lid.

Inside was a sculpture which, had any piece of sea glass existed large enough, must surely have been made from it. Its surface was cool beneath his palms as he lifted it out of the box. Rough-smooth, patinaed with just the same silky feeling of time and constant impact he loved in the pieces he picked up from the beach, picked up and left behind, no matter how rich and appealing their colours. The artist had somehow reproduced this in a single sweep of glass, one rich curve in shades that ran from indigo to jade across its surface. Holding it, Thomas wondered what it was supposed to represent, or how it was meant to stand up. He couldn't see any base to it. But when he set it on the table, it rocked a little, then seemed to take itself out of his grip and find its own centre of gravity, upon which it settled with perfect balance and weight. In doing so, it became what it was: a wave.

A perfect surfer's wave. Oh God. Flynn. Flynn, the chance encounter. The beautiful nutcase who should have left Thomas's mind as completely as he had left Porth Bay that morning, not leaving behind him a lonely pang, certainly not reviving himself inside the lighthouse fortress in the form of this absurdly beautiful gift.

Thomas sat down. The change of angle seemed to make the sculpture shift and murmur. It wasn't static. Had the power to bear out its creator's vision, not just once but every time it was observed. Unthinkingly he ran one finger over its crest, down into the beautifully evoked barrel. A lovely thing.

The trouble—one of the troubles; he did not dare even think about Flynn Summers' reasons for doing this, let alone how he was supposed to react—was that Thomas knew the artist. She ran a glassworks studio down in Marazion, overlooking St Michael's Mount, and her latest exhibition had so increased her reputation that the few pieces she produced in any year now cost a bloody fortune.

Thomas couldn't accept it, of course. It should have mortified him, that Flynn would even think the gesture necessary. It did. He was thoroughly embarrassed. He put his face into his hands and looked at the sculpture through his fingers. He felt the twitch of his own inexplicable smile against his palms.

Towards midnight, he took Belle outside for a last breath of air. There was still a trace of light on the western horizon—soon it would be summer. The pile of round white quartz stones gleamed on the turf. Feeling in his pocket, Thomas realised that, for the first time, he had failed to bring another from the beach to add to it. Yesterday the omission would have triggered in him a spasm of guilt and grief. He could not work out why, tonight, he did not mind. On his way back in, he chucked the glass of vodka down the sink.

***

That night Thomas dreamed. The dream of an ordinary man, for him so extraordinary that it woke him up smiling. No gunfire, no bloodstained dust. A pair of green eyes, full of wry laughter. Bronze-coloured hair, drying to gold in the sun. Thomas found that he was hard beneath his own caressing hand.

His libido was so uncertain and suppressed—another self-diagnosed and unacknowledged symptom—that he had not dared risk the briefest sexual encounter. Even alone, his hungers seldom went beyond an ache in his gut—unsatisfiable, unreachable yearnings inside the caudal curve of his spine. A painless arousal like this was too rare, too good, to let go, and Thomas rode the wave. The night was warm. He threw aside the cotton sheet under which he'd been sleeping, and knew a ripple of shock at the sight of his own naked self in the moonlight falling through the seaward window, his own erect cock, swelling as he grasped it. "God," he whispered, feeling his buttocks tighten, a slow heave of tension run through his whole body. He wanted to thrust into his hand, use himself freely and hard, and just…

He came, crying out in astonishment. Too soon, too wild. Tiny thoughts like bats or moths flitted on the edge of his mind— the sheets, the uncontrolled mess of his semen pouring down the back of his hand. Shuddering, he forced them aside, rolled over onto his belly and thrust with all his strength into the orgasm, hips pumping, his own grasp hot and firm. He had a moment, afterward, of painful loneliness—of fear, at falling asleep like this, soaked and disarrayed—but the release had been too thorough, and he slipped away before the dark could find him.

***

Next morning, the sculpture was still there, beautiful but out of place in Thomas Penrose's home. He possessed no ornament. The clean bare lines of his rooms suited him. He wasn't an ascetic, and could see how the deep bay of the living room's east window, let all the way through the thickness of the tower's walls, almost cried out for this lovely thing against its whitewashed stone, but he couldn't keep it. Any such constant reminder of an event which had been beyond his control would make him uneasy—and besides, there was no way he could accept so expensive a gift from a stranger. Thomas didn't know what they paid the RNAS rescue crews, but he was fairly sure their salaries didn't run to impulse buys like this. An impulse buy—yes, he could see the bright, sun-washed man he had met yesterday acting on a reflex of the recently saved—occasionally Thomas had patients do the same thing—but he was sure to be regretting it now.

It was Saturday morning, and Thomas found himself driving up towards the airbase, the sculpture packed away and safely stowed in the back. He didn't want to be rude or unappreciative. He would find Flynn, give the gift back to him personally. Tell him he'd just been doing his job.

RNAS Hawke Lake was vast, a sprawl of hangars and air towers that extended from the Helleskern cliffs to nearly four miles inland, encompassing on its western side the little town of Breagh, whose main purpose now was to serve the base. There were a few bleak rows of pebble-dashed houses on the town's outskirts which Thomas knew belonged to the military, and it was here that he thought Flynn might live. When he stopped to make enquiries at the post office, however, he was told that because Lieutenant Summers was a single man and relatively new arrival, he still lived on the base itself, within its barbed-wire perimeter.

The roads around Hawke were, of course, among the few really well-maintained rural highways in Cornwall, and Thomas drove back the way he had come, blinking in the brilliant April sun. He wasn't so sure of what he was doing now. He felt odd this morning, better than he had in some time, but sleepy and a bit spaced out. The road's slow curve around the base was hypnotic, free of the potholes that kept him awake and alert everywhere else, the Rover's tyres whispering on its smooth surface. He knew military bases painfully well, and even as he pulled up outside the main entrance, with its barriers and flanking guard posts, was aware that he wasn't going to get very far. The sensible thing to do would have been to go back home, stow the sculpture carefully under the stairs and wait until he ran into Flynn by chance somewhere.

He couldn't have it back in the house, even boxed and invisible. Thomas knew, his sleepy contentment burning off from him, that it had become a focal point. He hated himself for the reaction, feared, though, that next time his control slipped he would end up pitching the beautiful thing off the cliff. Sighing, he took the box from the back seat and approached the barriers, trying to look as unconcerned and as little like a terrorist as he could. Everyone everywhere was on permanent high alert, it seemed, even here.

No, he could not have access to Lieutenant Summers. No, the guard would not phone the barracks—the lieutenant was on duty and could not be disturbed. Thomas, standing stiff-spined in the sunshine, felt the beginnings of rage—it was just this routine, knee-jerk hostility that had begun to disgust him with military life. It forced him to be on his dignity to meet it. Here, face-to-face with this stuffed-shirt sergeant, he was no longer the respected village doctor but an interloper, a supplicant.

A couple of Navy ratings were leaning on the bonnet of a jeep, watching the encounter with amusement. One of them gave Thomas a grinning once-over. He turned to his companion and said, broad Belfast accent pitched to carry, "Looks like flyin' Flynn's been playin' away. Doc had better watch out for Rob Tremaine, eh?"

One useful side effect of Thomas's condition was sudden and complete emotional cutoff under pressure. At another time, he might have cared or wondered who Rob Tremaine was. As things were, he shrugged. He took a couple of steps back from the guard and, moving slowly so as to make his intentions quite clear and avert any hair-trigger reactions, laid the box on the ground. "This is for Flynn Summers," he said flatly. "It came to me by mistake. Check it for wires and detonate it if you have to. Otherwise, make sure he gets it." He turned away. He wished he had Belle with him—she covered his rear, and gave good withering backward glances—but did not think he made a bad job of his exit.

Chapter Three
Crosscurrents

It was like pins and needles, like waking up with your arm folded under you. The numbness was bad, but things were briefly worse when it wore off.

By the time he got back home, Thomas was mortified by his own lack of grace. His courtesy was deeper ingrained in him even than the scars of his combat experience, and returning Flynn's gift like that was far from what he had intended. He flinched to think of the way in which Flynn might get his parcel back. *Some bloke dropped this off for you. Said he didn't want it.* Followed up, probably, by *Don't have your bloody packages delivered through the gate, Lieutenant. We're not the Royal Mail.*

He struggled to put the whole mess out of his mind. It was over, and a good lesson to him in not allowing random elements into his life. Probably he would never see Flynn again, and if he had offended him, what was the harm? *But what if you've hurt him,* the undamaged parts of Thomas whispered, making him shiver and become abstracted when conducting routine medical checks, taking temperatures, listening to nicotine-clogged chests. That was ridiculous, though. It had been a half-hour encounter, and

Summers had probably since then faced death several times on the open seas, winching stranded fishermen to safety. He wasn't going to care about some imagined slight from a man whose name he had likely forgotten by now. In all probability he was simply relieved that he'd got away with it, not had his mad impulse taken to heart.

Still, it nagged at Thomas. He seemed to notice the passage of the Sea King helicopters overhead, with their distinctive grey and red livery, far more intensely than he had ever done before. By the following Saturday, he liked himself even less than usual, and instead of spending his day in the stern isolation that went some way towards repairing the social exhaustion of his week, he packed up the Land Rover, wolfhound and all, and drove down to the Perran Beach air show.

He'd never attended such an event before. Like any other kid he had watched the choppers plying the Cornish skies on their missions and imagined himself up there, but had felt no interest beyond that. He wasn't really interested now. Any fascination with helicopter travel he might have been harbouring had been thoroughly knocked out of him by his first few Chinook flights over hostile terrain in Helmand Province.

He stood, beached and a little disoriented, beside the Land Rover, parked in a field among the hundreds of other cars, mobile homes and Volksie buses glittering in the sun. Occasionally he would spot acquaintances in the crowd and exchange a smile with them, wryly noting their surprise at seeing him there.

Glancing round at Belle, he saw that she was wearing her most haughty mask. Anyone who didn't know her would think her unfriendly. For the first time, it occurred to Thomas to think about his own image—the effect he produced on others. He wasn't unfriendly, either, but not one of the people who caught his eye and smiled at him came up to say hello. For the first time, he found himself minding.

A thunderous reverberation on the edge of the world distracted him, and he leaned on the Rover and watched the display. Six Sea King helicopters and four military Lynxes, the full Hawke Lake and Plymouth complement, breached the horizon in tight formation. The sight was oddly moving, Thomas had to admit, as long as he kept in mind their lifesaving remit and forgot that they also bore down mercilessly, with fully armed crews, on the gun- and drug-runners who often made a dash along the Cornish coast. Perhaps what touched him was the brotherhood implicit in their close-quarters flight. What faith you must have, in yourself and your comrades, to spin those double sets of thin, flashing blades so close to those of the surrounding craft, to fly almost flank to flank.

He listened to the announcer trying to give the crowd a commentary through the wind and rotor roar. Their pilots were trained, he said, to maintain steady height relative to a forty-foot pitching ocean swell, to compensate for hurricane-force winds. Each of the Sea Kings was fifty-five feet long, weighed in at six tons, could reach speeds of one hundred forty miles per hour...

It should have been hard to imagine Flynn, who stayed in Thomas's memory as a bright-haired sea spirit, strapped into the cockpit of one of these vast machines, putting it through its manoeuvres. Although there was considerable grace in the flight of the Sea Kings, it was massive, ponderous, a great industrial pod of metal-clad whales on the move. Last year the Red Arrow fighter jets had flown over Perran for the air show, to the pride of the local council—their aerobatic displays had a formidable waiting list. Thomas hadn't seen them, but had caught them from a distance as they swooped, converged and exploded apart with a surfer's nonchalant flair. Yes, he could see Flynn as a jet pilot.

Giving it thought, though, he had surprisingly little trouble putting him at the Sea King's controls too. He would be capable and fast, his body braced against the vibe of the machine…

When Thomas's mind delivered the image of Flynn's tanned and elegant hand closing firmly on the Sea King's joystick, he astounded himself with a shout of laughter. *Oh my God.* Time to go home, definitely. He was not quite sure what he had come here to accomplish, but the chopper team was landing now in neat formation on the tarmac a couple of hundred yards away. The display was over. Belle was looking at him in bewilderment, and he had turned a few heads among the spectators around him too.

He turned to open the Land Rover's door and saw that, while he had been staring at helicopters like a ten-year-old boy, he had been neatly and shamelessly parked in. A Volkswagen camper, typically, painted end to end with flowers and peace signs. Thomas looked for the driver, but he was nowhere to be seen. Probably hadn't even noticed the Land Rover and two other vehicles he had paralysed. Bloody hippies.

Thomas felt a cold twist of anger, which was more to do with being trapped than inconvenienced. Now he would have to find his way across the field to the tannoy tent and get a bloody announcement made, like a lost child.

Then he stopped. What the hell was his problem? The day was warm, the wind soft. It was May, he suddenly realised. Over at Padstow, the 'Obby 'Oss dancers would have made their ancient rites to welcome the summer, scattering blossoms across half of Cornwall and scaring maiden tourists to death with the terrible old hobbyhorse, whose operative made it ceremonially bite as many unsuspecting backsides as he possibly could. Thomas used to love the Padstow rites. Why hadn't he gone?

Running a hand across his hair, he felt himself calming, the old gift of perspective returning to him. Was his time so precious, his day so packed with duties, that he had to go running off to demand his release? And as far as bloody hippies were concerned, there were worse things to be parked in by. Thomas knew he should be grateful, and found that he actually was. A kid's Volksie bus, not a Snatch Land Rover or armoured truck. The roar of slowing rotors just the coda to a good day out, not a signal that within ten minutes he would be up to his elbows in the blood of incoming wounded. He had his usual flask of decent coffee on the back seat. There was no hurry.

He set the flask on the roof, and then on impulse scrambled up to join it, a trick he hadn't practised in a while. He was relieved that he was still agile enough for the jump, as well as that the Rover's creaking metalwork would still bear his weight. He could see across the whole paddock from here. Pouring himself a coffee, he idly took in the stalls and marquees, the bright flap of bunting, the blessed multicoloured clash of civilian garments in a peaceful crowd. Yes, there were worse places he could be.

Belle, who had been watching him in approval, suddenly stood up and issued one of her rare barks. Thomas looked down at her, smiling and frowning. She was becoming quite demonstrative in her old age. She began a slow, dignified circling, which Thomas after a long time had learned to interpret as anticipation of some desired person or event.

"What's the matter with you?" he asked her, and, shielding his eyes against the sun, looked out over the field again.

The helicopter crews had disembarked. It might have been a display flight only, but they were fully kitted up in their rescue gear, the orange jumpsuits, designed to be visible at sea, almost incandescent in the sunlight. Not hard to spot, as they dispersed in small groups among the crowd, attracting hordes of excited kids.

Thomas repressed a grin. There were certainly two kinds of old-blood Cornishmen—his own type, stocky and dark, who had probably been here as long as the rocks, and the Bronze Age Celts who had succeeded them, strapping creatures, often blonds or redheads, with piercing blue-grey eyes. The six-foot-odd example of the latter breed standing regally in the crowd almost made Thomas laugh again, he was such a perfect picture. Thomas could imagine his own ancestors apprehensively watching from their green mounds while these invaders made landfall from many-oared boats. Red-gold hair, bright as metal in the breeze, plainly lapping up the attention from the hero-worshipping children around him too, bending down like a film star to give autographs.

Thomas blinked. To the left of this Bronze Age giant, hanging back a bit and somehow eclipsed by him, was Flynn Summers. Thomas, who was now aware that he had been thinking of little else all week, was astonished that he hadn't noticed him. It was as if his companion somehow put his lights out, somehow made him look ordinary. He seemed to be chatting distractedly to one little boy, but every so often he lifted his head and scanned the crowd, as if looking for something or anxious to be somewhere else. On the next of these wistful surveys, his eye caught Thomas's.

He blazed up again. Thomas saw once more his brilliant smile, the sea-green brightening of his gaze. Involuntarily Thomas glanced over his shoulder—surely this lovely reillumination couldn't be for him—but there was nobody else sitting on top of a truck around here, consciously or otherwise making himself noticeable. Diffidently he raised a hand in greeting, and saw Flynn touch the other man's arm and gesture towards him.

He dismounted from his perch, resisting the urge to tug his shirt straight or check in the wing mirror that his hair had not performed its occasional trick of standing up in spikes across his crown. This was, for God's sake, the most casual acquaintance imaginable—thirty minutes, ten of which they had both spent trying not to drown. Belle increased the pace of her circling, then suddenly peeled off and, to Thomas's surprise, went confidently trotting down between the line of cars to greet Flynn as he approached.

Thomas was so absurdly glad to see him that, for a moment, his voice wouldn't work. He put out a hand awkwardly—their introductions had already been made, but he could hardly go up and embrace him, much as some idiotic part of him wanted to. Much as, strangely, Flynn looked as if he would have liked to return the gesture. Both settled for a brief, fervent handclasp. "Hi," Thomas managed. He looked at Belle, now standing at Flynn's side as if she belonged to him, or vice versa. "My dog seems to like you. Which is weird, because she doesn't like anybody."

Flynn smiled. "Great place for her to start—with the bloke who tried to drown her master, I mean. How are you?"

"Fine. How have you been?" Automatically Thomas found himself glancing at the healing scratches on Flynn's brow and cheek. "No colds, or…"

Flynn broke into laughter. Helplessly Thomas reflected that it was one of the nicest sounds he'd ever heard—generous and natural as the sunlit wind. "Fine, Dr. Thomas. How's your shoulder? Any sign of rabies?"

Thomas found that he was grinning back. It felt good to be resisted like this. Even the healthiest and least self-centred of men seemed to feel the need to detail their little aches and pains when asked how they were by the local GP, and he in turn would use his role in place of conversation. "No. Not yet, anyway. Look, Flynn, I'm glad I saw you. I…"

A shadow fell. Belle shifted and subtly turned herself round so that she was shielding both Thomas and Flynn. For a wonder, she emitted a low growl, and Thomas took her firmly by the collar as the six-foot Celt emerged from between two cars. *My ancient enemy*, he thought, smiling at the lurid concept, and stepped forward as Flynn, who had for some reason gone a little pale, said, "Oh, hi, Rob. Robert Tremaine, this is Thomas Penrose, the doctor up at Sankerris. My saviour from the other week."

The new arrival looked Thomas over. At first his expression did not indicate any particular pleasure at the introduction or the idea of the rescue. He had a striking, raw-boned face on which contempt would sit easily. Then he smiled, a wide bright flash only slightly marred by predatory, overlarge teeth, and thrust out a hand. "Ah," he greeted Thomas warmly. "Flynn told me what happened. Pleased to meet you. I owe you a great deal."

For a moment, Thomas tried to misunderstand him. Why, he didn't know. There was less than no reason for the ache of disappointment trying to begin in him, the slight strained tightness in his throat. What had he been thinking? Tremaine slung his arm around Flynn's shoulders, drew him close in to his side and briefly ruffled his hair, and there was no room left for confusion. No need, either, for this great strapping airman to be scent-marking his territory, which was what it looked to Thomas for all the world like he was trying to do. What had Flynn said to him? Or was this just a general warning display, put on for all passing males, however unlikely they were as potential competition? Whatever was going on, poor Flynn looked mortified. Time for some inane, normalising conversation. Thomas thought he could just about remember how to do that.

He shook Tremaine's hand briskly. "Good to meet you too. That was quite a display up there. You and Flynn are cracking pilots."

And somehow that was wrong. Perhaps his small talk was rustier than he'd feared. Flynn's pallor had deepened. "Oh," he said, smiling sheepishly. "Robert's the pilot, not me. I'm just crew. The tea bag."

Thomas frowned. "The what?"

"Means we tie him to a rope end and dip him in the water," Tremaine clarified, giving Flynn a squeeze. "Flynn's the business end. Harder job by far."

Thomas could believe it. He'd seen a couple of rescues, when he'd gone out in the lifeboat to help with the survivors, and had wondered at the nerve of the men who got winched down into the heaving waters, tied to their friends, their craft and their lives by one thin umbilical. If Flynn was ashamed, he had no reason. He'd never claimed to be a pilot.

"Right," Thomas said, not certain how to go on. "Well, it was an amazing sight. I…"

Flynn smiled, visibly deciding to help him out. "Wow. Did you come on purpose to see us?" He looked around, saw the camper van and grinned. "Oh, no. You just couldn't escape."

"No, I got parked in. But I did come to see you, actually." This was Thomas's chance. He could have done without Robert's assessing grey gaze on him, but it couldn't be helped. "I wanted to say I was sorry for dropping off the parcel like that. I meant to give it back to you, but—"

"It's all right."

Not a reassurance—a cutoff, a plea that he didn't go on. Thomas, never slow to pick up on human distress cues, closed his mouth. Too late, of course. The grey eyes had acquired a curious lupine sheen. In retrospect Thomas could see it had been tactless of him, trying to allay his own anxieties like that—Tremaine did not look like the kind of lover who would tolerate…

"Hoi!" Tremaine abruptly yelled, making Belle raise her hackles. He was looking off between the parked cars. Following his gaze, Thomas saw a skinny teenager approaching through the crowd, a pretty long-haired girlfriend hanging on one arm, the other stacked high with secondhand books, CDs and a stuffed giraffe from the tombola stall. "Yes, you, you inconsiderate little shit," Tremaine continued, as the poor lad noticed him. "Do you realise you're stopping a very busy doctor from reaching his patients?"

The boy, ashen, broke into a trot, scattering belongings on the turf. "Oh God," Thomas said. "Don't, Robert. I'm not on duty." But even if Tremaine had heard him, which he doubted, he was too late—the kids were pelting in what looked like sheer terror for their van. The boy skidded to a halt for one second, staying well out of range of the formidable airman in his glaring orange flight suit.

"Sorry, dude!" he shouted to Thomas, jumped into the Volksie and roared off as fast as the clustered vehicles and pitted field would allow.

Tremaine turned back to face him. He was beaming from ear to ear, having apparently thoroughly enjoyed the exercise of frightening children. "There you go," he said to Thomas. "Bloody hippies, eh?" Thomas, who'd inwardly expressed the same sentiment not half an hour before, felt a sudden sense of affinity for them. Flynn, too, looked as if he would rather have been on the bus. "Right. You can go about your business, Doctor. And we have to go about ours, flyin' Flynn—time we warmed the birds up for the four o'clock. Bye, Thomas. Nice meeting you."

Thomas elected not to watch them leave. He tried to define for himself the pain it would have cost him to do so. Partly it was just the chagrin of being walked off on, a mild humiliation he could avoid by turning his back and going about his business. And in part, he realised, it was his reluctance to see Flynn hustled off. He did not want to think about Rob Tremaine doing that. Did not want to envisage Flynn allowing it to be done.

He was packing up the Land Rover when a warm grip fastened on his arm. His nerves were raw from his encounter with Tremaine—this was, he had reminded himself grimly, why he avoided people in general—and he repressed a violent flinch. But it was only Flynn. His grasp was tight, electrical. "Thomas," he began urgently. "I'm sorry about that. Rob's okay, just... Listen. I've only got a second. There's no hard feelings over the package. Really. I wanted you to have it, but I always go too bloody far. Look, will you come and join us for a drink in the Fox tonight? To say thank you, since you won't accept my crazy offerings? It'll just be me and the lads. Please?"

Thomas opened his mouth to refuse. *What am I meant to do with you and the lads in a bloody airbase pub?* But Flynn bestowed on him a smile of such persuasive sweetness that the protest melted on his lips. "We'll be there around seven," he said. They both stood in silence for a moment. Thomas could not have said what they were waiting for. Flynn, still smiling, was interrogating his gaze, brow furrowing, lower lip caught in his teeth. He looked almost hopeful—and thoroughly confused. When the shifting wind brought rotor roar to them once more, he let go Thomas's arm with a faint, near-guilty start. "I've got to get back," he murmured, and turning away, set off at a jog through the crowd. Steadying himself on the Rover's wing mirror, Thomas watched him go.

***

He had no idea what to wear. He worried about it briefly, staring into a seldom-used full-length mirror in his bedroom, then shook his head in impatience. Suppose he dressed up, who would that be for? Flynn was—comprehensively—taken, and even had it been otherwise, Thomas could not imagine a world in which their lives could possibly converge. He was damaged goods, a battered war vet with OCD and an incipient booze problem. He wouldn't lay a hand on Flynn's bright young life, even if he could.

Clean and reasonably well-ironed would have to do. Thomas took one of his white linen shirts out of the wardrobe in which hung five others exactly like it and issued himself one of five sets of identical black cords. He checked that Belle had water, biscuits and her favourite rubber toy, and apologised to her—she was no more prepared than he was for him to be spending an evening out.

Out, for God's sake, with a wild bunch of RNAS flyboys and hotshots, and Robert Tremaine, who for all his bonhomie and surface charm, would plainly have liked to deck him at the fairground that afternoon.

Thomas smiled wryly. Flynn wanted him there, and he owed him one friendly act. Then it would be over.

***

Over before it started, almost. Thomas walked into the Fox in Breagh village and nearly turned and walked straight out again. The racket hit him like a brick. He realised with a shock how long it had been since he had ventured into even the quietest of pubs, and this place was rocking, U2 blasting out of the speakers, the unrestrained shouting and laughter of military men off duty. A few beleaguered women too, Thomas noted, making his way through the crowd, although they also looked as if they belonged to the base.

The whole place had more the air of an army canteen than a Cornish bar. It was modern, and utilitarian in structure, harsh neon lights glaring. Pretty horrible, really, he wryly reflected, asking himself once again—as he had half a dozen times on the road down from his lonely, sea-swept coast—why he had accepted Flynn's invitation. Now he was here—and his arrival hadn't gone unnoticed, a few heads turning to check out the civilian entering the RNAS den—he would have to make a decent show of it. He'd timed his arrival for half an hour later than Flynn's estimated seven o'clock, in the hope of not getting there first, but it didn't seem to have worked.

Had he always been like this? Diffident, barely able to hold his head up in a noisy crowd? Suddenly Thomas was annoyed with himself. Probably he laid too much at the door of his experiences in Helmand. Yes, he'd always been shy. But he'd had the grace to hide it, to reach back to offered friendliness. It didn't really matter that Flynn wasn't here. And this might be a Navy pub, but they didn't own it and could just put up with him while he had a drink at the bar like a normal person.

A warmth at his elbow. Thomas felt it through the rolled-back sleeve of his shirt. He turned around, smiling. *Yes.*

"I didn't think you'd come."

The room was very warm. Thomas wondered if that had set the colour under Flynn's tan, but as he watched, it faded. God, was this still a world in which he could make someone flush with pleasure at his arrival? He pushed the idea away. Flynn could just as well have been regretting the invitation, embarrassed that he had turned up.

"Well," Thomas said. "I wanted to talk to you. I didn't get the chance to explain, about the sculpture."

It was strange, he thought. The crush at the bar was one shade off a rugby scrum, but it felt as if the two of them were quite alone. He doubted the harried bartender would ever notice them, especially since neither he nor Flynn seemed able to spare attention to catch his eye. He had managed to commandeer a barstool, and Flynn had squeezed in beside him so that they were elbow-to-elbow on the beer-soaked formica surface.

"You don't have to. I was down in Marazion that afternoon, and I must've still had water on my brain—not because I bought you something, I mean. To go over the top and embarrass you."

"Oh, it didn't. At least…" Thomas shook his head. "Not in that way, though I know how much those pieces cost. I meant to return it to you personally, to explain. Then things went a bit…" he searched for an expression to convey the debacle at the Hawke Lake barricade, "…a bit pear-shaped, and I ended up dumping it with the guard on the main gate. I'm sorry."

Flynn laughed. "I can imagine the scene. In fact, Junior Seaman Davis described it in detail when he brought the parcel to my barracks. He said you looked ready to take on the whole airbase, one man at a time. They're silly bastards. Forget about them." A movement in the crowd threatened to knock Thomas off his barstool, and Flynn stretched out a warning hand to shield him. "Christ, what a bunch of thugs. We'll go somewhere quieter in a minute. Just…just tell me one thing. Did you like it?"

"What?" Thomas asked stupidly. He had been too caught up in watching his companion's easy grace. He'd seen him so far in a wetsuit and an unbecoming orange flying kit. In his civvies—just a black T-shirt and jeans, but outlining every plane and curve of his shoulders, his hips—he was distracting. Like the sculpture, pleasing from all angles. Renewing his charm with each motion. "Oh, the… Yes. I loved it, actually. Was it okay? Could you return it all right?"

"Er… Yes. Yes, sure. Come on, let me get you a drink. What'll you have?"

"Thanks. Just an orange, please."

"You'll need more than that to get you through a night with this lot."

Thomas glanced round him at the pandemonium, smiling. "Probably, but I'm driving."

"You can still have one."

"No, I can't." Thomas kept his smile in place, but felt Flynn's attention refocus upon him—a quick, gentle concern, a warm readiness of perception he hardly knew how to bear. He did not want to tell this new friend that *just one*, on a night like this, would trigger the next fifteen or so, and maybe Flynn knew already—had heard in the village shop that the Sankerris GP sometimes went on discreet, off-duty three-day benders. Struggling to keep it light, he said, with mock solemnity, "I'm a doctor, Flynn. It's my job to preserve life."

"Yes, but not in bloody formaldehyde, Doc!" A big hand landed on Thomas's shoulder. He jumped, hard, and felt Flynn move imperceptibly to steady him. Rob Tremaine had erupted from the crowd behind them, grinning maniacally, plainly three sheets to the wind. "Bill," he yelled to the bartender, who dropped a glass as if it had scalded him and abandoned the customer he'd been serving. "Pint for me and for Flynn, and make the doc's a screwdriver. And bring them out the back, for God's sake—I can't hear myself think in this circus."

The pub had a small beer garden, more of a yard, fenced around with concrete-poured walls similar to the ones that enclosed the airbase. Security concerns, Thomas wondered, trailing Rob and Flynn outside, or maybe an attempt to shield the neighbouring houses.

"Is it always like this?" he asked, watching Tremaine steer Flynn to a table, a proprietorial hand planted on his spine, aware that, if he did not take care, he would find himself disliking Tremaine intensely.

Flynn glanced round at him, smiling wryly, perhaps reading the thought. "No. Special occasion. Birthday."

"Oh." Thomas took a seat at the wooden trestle. He thought that Tremaine, settling opposite, would have pulled Flynn onto his lap if he could. Fine with Thomas, if Flynn had not looked uncomfortable, stiff with resistance in his grasp. "Yours?"

"No, mine," Tremaine boomed, lifting his pint. "Cheers, lads. Drink up. No, Flynnie here's a February baby, a merry..." He trailed off suddenly, as if catching himself about to commit a faux pas.

"A merrybegot?" Thomas finished for him. He had knocked back his drink without noticing, and could feel the familiar dangerous sparkle in his blood. That *was* old Cornish. And now that he'd listened to him for a while, Tremaine was hiding a good old West Country drawl beneath his officer-class RP. Come to think of it, Thomas recognised the name. Recognised *him*, he thought.

"A merrybegot's a baby conceived in May," he explained to Flynn, who was looking bewildered. "Off in the greenwood after a Beltane ceremony." He gave Flynn a smile from which he could not hide a trace of tenderness. "They'd arrive in February, with the lambs. Considered blessed by the gods. Robert, you've got to be one of the old Sankerris Bay Tremaines, to know that."

Robert stared at him. Thomas hadn't meant to take the wind from his sails, but he wasn't sorry to see it go. "Yeah," he said, then, clearly regretting the unguarded response, "No. That is, I am, but from the London branch. Moved away from here to make money centuries ago and never looked back."

Thomas let it go, but he found he was amused. Plainly this great sophisticated airman was scabby little Bobby Tremaine, descendant of a family of notorious seventeenth-century moonrakers. Thomas should know, having not only treated the current little scions of the race for fleas and malnutrition, and arranged social care where necessary, but being descended himself from an equally infamous rival smuggling gang, whose territory had overlapped theirs, with violent results. Penroses and Tremaines, fighting tooth and claw for contraband, luring ships to their doom on the rocks of Sankerris cove. He used to run the streets with Bobby, although even then, with the ruthless pack instincts of childhood, he and his friends had distanced themselves from the Bay kids, their poverty and disasters. You'd play with them, but not invite them home. The family face was distinct. Thomas wondered why Tremaine was lying.

Ashamed of his old prejudices, his readiness to judge, Thomas smiled at him. He was the last person to object, if someone had chosen some other life than the one he'd been born with. "Well," he said. "Happy birthday. I'll go and get a round in."

By the time he got back, Rob and Flynn were nowhere to be seen. He set the drinks on the trestle table, reflecting grimly how much easier it had been to thread the crowd and make his presence known at the bar with even one shot of alcohol inside him, how much easier still to get back if he'd magicked his second orange juice into a screwdriver too. What had stopped him was the knowledge that, if he did, he'd have to find somewhere in Breagh to spend the night. What he did to himself was his own business, but there the harm stopped.

He seemed to have lost his hosts anyway. Well, Tremaine had looked ready to drag Flynn off to his lair. Thomas's stomach lurched at the thought, but he told himself that he was relieved. He could get out of here now.

There was an archway to the left of the doors back into the pub. Thomas thought it led to the toilets and then through to the front and the car park. A delicate May dusk had fallen, a violet cobweb behind the glaring white arc light the pub management was keeping trained on the outdoor revellers. The entrance to the passage was stark black in its shadow, from this angle at least. To those better placed at the other tables scattered around the yard, whatever it held was apparently of some interest, and as Thomas drew closer, he picked up the distinct sound of an argument begun in discreet whispers, starting to escalate to shouts.

Well, Tremaine was shouting. Flynn's voice was in there—trying, Thomas thought, to make a point—but he was still sober, and his low-voiced fervour wasn't carrying against the tide. Thomas heard, *who does he think*, and *what did you bring him here for*, and did his very best to stop listening. None of his business, even if Rob was doing his best to make it that way, and he didn't want to add to the performance. Flynn and Tremaine were drawing enough attention on their own. Glancing round the crowd, Thomas saw a few benign smiles, as if this might be a regular sideshow on airbase nights out, but only a few. The older men—higher-ranking officers, presumably—looked grim in a way that did not promise any good to Rob's career or Flynn's. Locking his gaze to the ground, Thomas took his jacket off the trestle bench and checked for his car keys. Definitely time for him to go.

A gasp from the archway's shadows. It wouldn't have slowed Thomas down, except that he wouldn't have thought Flynn could sound like that. Outraged, yes, and that was the bulk of the message. But under it—tiny, fleeting, a flash Thomas wondered if he'd imagined. Yes, fear.

Flynn, though elegant, looked tough as nails. Nobody's pushover. For Thomas, that abruptly made it worse. What the hell hold did Rob have on him? Dropping his coat, he strode over to the passageway entrance, ignoring the hoots and warning shouts from the crowd.

Okay, that kind of hold. Not unexpected, though he could hardly believe Tremaine had been mad enough to try it here. He was grasping Flynn by the hair at the back of his neck, and if he'd got away with one forced kiss, Flynn was definitely not having any of the next. His hands were planted flat to Tremaine's chest.

Without conscious thought on the subject, Thomas decided enough was enough. He grabbed Rob's shoulder. "Hoi," he said, his own old Cornish burr rising through his manners and his surgery veneer. "Flynn, is this bastard bothering you?"

Tremaine spun on him with a snarl. Thomas was surprised at the purity of hatred on his face. Flynn, released, almost fell over. "Shit," he gasped. "Thomas, for God's sake. Get out of here. I can handle him."

Of course he can. That was what he got for interfering—Flynn looked, if possible, even more mortified now than before. Thomas raised both hands. "Great. Do that. Handle him, please."

He turned to go. A vast weight landed on his back. Without an instant's thought, he ducked, uncurled and sent Rob Tremaine flying over his shoulder to crash in a flail of arms and legs in the courtyard.

A roar of laughter went up. Thomas didn't think it was funny. He had no idea he'd remembered his unarmed-combat training, let alone that he'd be willing to use it on a helpless drunk. *First, do no harm…* He glanced at Flynn, whose face was still a white blank of shock. Self-disgust tore at him. He had got into a public brawl within half an hour of starting his first social endeavour in years.

He went to crouch by Tremaine, automatically beginning diagnostic checks—that his head wasn't damaged, that his pupils were the same size. "I'm sorry," he said. "You startled me. Are you hurt?"

Tremaine's big fist shot up and fastened in the front of his shirt.

Once more, Thomas unreflectingly blocked the move, as he had with dozens of soldiers who'd grasped at him in extremity before he could get drugs into them. Rob's eyes blazed into his.

What was the problem here? Yes, he'd caught him mid-tussle with Flynn, but it was hardly as if half his division hadn't been watching that too. Christ, was it because he'd recognised him? It couldn't be the first time for that, either, but Flynn was new to the district. Maybe Robert had told him a different story. "Stop it. Are you hurt?"

"What the fuck do you care?"

"The bare bloody minimum, in your case. But I'm a doctor."

"Oh, yeah." Tremaine relaxed his grip and fell back, sneering. "Right. I know you too, *Doctor*. Up in your ivory tower, drinking yourself to death. No girlfriend, no missus. Queer as fuck, I shouldn't wonder. Well, you chose the wrong night to crawl out and have a grab at my Flynn."

"Oh, for…" Thomas sat back on his heels. He refused to turn and look around the courtyard, which had fallen silent to listen. He couldn't blame them. He had lived a quiet life, detached. Probably perceived as aloof. Their attention to this total and sudden exposure felt like hammer-blows to bruised skin. Flynn had stumbled over and crouched on Tremaine's other side, his face ashen. Thomas couldn't meet his eyes.

"Rob, please," Flynn said unsteadily. "You're pissed. Thomas hasn't done anything to you. Let us help you up, and we'll go home."

"Don't need any fucking help," Tremaine growled, and rolled lithely to his feet. Thomas braced not to take a reflexive step back—or, which he was gathering would have been worse, a step to shield Flynn. He was bemused at the impulse. Tremaine was big, but Flynn's ability to take care of himself declared itself in every leanly muscled inch.

The three of them stood staring at one another, a grim impasse Thomas was at a loss to know how to end. He'd just have walked away from it, had not Flynn's distress latched itself into his heart, exerting an inexplicable steel-cable tug despite all the disasters being with him seemed to attract. "It's all right," he said to Flynn softly, and reaching a hand to his shoulder, made his last mistake.

Tremaine slammed him up against the courtyard wall. If he heard Flynn's shout or felt his restraining grip, he gave no sign. "Right!" he bellowed, nose an inch from Thomas's. "I tell you what—you can *have* the little fucker. Good luck with him. Good luck with the nightmares and the novel fucking ways he comes up with of committing fucking suicide every other fucking week. Ask him why he doesn't fly anymore. You'll be a lovely bloody pair, actually—the fuck-up pilot and the alcoholic village quack."

He let Thomas go. Turned, and began to walk off. Thomas watched, immobile. Everything had started going very slow, an underwater sensation he recognised. For once he welcomed the symptoms of oncoming fugue. Like Flynn's wave, the seventh wave, it would carry him out of here, what was left of his dignity intact. He would hear and see little, drive home efficiently, go to bed… Voices came oddly to him, distorting, crackling. He could see Flynn's face, also near to his now. He felt the warm brush of Flynn's palm down his cheek, almost heard his shocked, pleading voice. *Thomas, don't listen. I'm so sorry.*

What was he sorry for? Thomas looked at him for a moment. It was almost a shame that in a second's time the cold would come down on him, extinguishing everything—rage, which he could do without, and even the exquisite pleasure of that soothing touch. He waited.

It didn't happen.

"Robert," he said, low, smooth as silk. Tremaine was nearly at the door, but he turned. Thomas stepped up to him. He drew back his fist, gave the other man time to see it, to know his intention, and belted him as hard as he could in the face.

Tremaine went down—decisively this time—and this time Dr. Penrose did not care if he cracked his thick skull like a melon.

***

He eased the Land Rover carefully out of its space. He was stone-cold sober now, the alcohol metabolised off in the adrenaline still blazing through his system. The knuckles of his left hand were bleeding. He had disgraced himself, absolutely. He felt wonderful. Had he raised a brief, startled cheer from the watching crowd? He wasn't sure. Didn't care. He felt as if he'd punched the face of every army bigot who had ever called him queer, every supercilious public-school major-general who thought that doctors had an easy berth on the front line. Better still, every fear of his own that had been twisting up his life since his return. His heart was pounding. Drawing deep breaths, he wound down the window to gasp the night air, which was cool now, smelling of sea salt and freedom, and pulled out onto the road.

Movement in his rearview mirror. For an instant he thought that Tremaine might have followed him, and shuddered at the inward roar of anticipation the prospect caused. Easing off the gas, he let the Rover's engine idle.

Flynn appeared at the window, his hair disordered, breath coming ragged. "Thomas. Wait a second. Please."

Thomas pulled up the handbrake. He watched as Flynn laid a hand on the window to steady himself, opened his mouth as if to explain. Then he visibly gave up and lowered his head so that his brow was resting on the back of his hand. "Oh God."

Thomas looked at him. Whatever Tremaine's power over him, it could throw him into utter disarray. His breath was coming far harder and more ragged than his run from the pub could account for, and the knuckles of the hand Thomas could see were clenched white. "Are you okay?"

"Yes. Yes, but…that was the worst social occasion of my entire bloody life."

Thomas considered. He would have liked to say something to make him feel better, and cast back over his own bloody life to see if he could remember anything worse. He came up dry. "Yeah," he agreed, after a few seconds. "Mine too. What's his problem, Flynn?"

"Whatever it is, will you at least believe that it's my fault as much as his?"

The street was quiet. Its single light caught shades of bronze in Flynn's hair. His bowed head was eloquent of something approaching desperation, surrender. Thomas resisted, and then did not resist, the urge to caress it, and Flynn looked up in surprise. "Whatever you say. Is he all right?"

"Yes, he… He's fine."

"Good. Do you want me to run you back to the base? Give him some time to cool off on his own?"

Flynn laughed tiredly. "My address is bunk two, room six of the west barrack. His is bunk one. Will you just drop me off at the B&B in Boskenna? It's on your way home."

Thomas thought, with fear and repulsion, of Flynn encountering Tremaine again tonight. Boskenna didn't seem far enough—and, as the only accommodation for miles around, not much of a secret bolthole. "Get in," he said, and when Flynn had clambered up into the passenger seat beside him, he gave the wheel a thoughtful tap and turned to him. "Would it cause a diplomatic incident if you came home with me?"

"What, another one?" Flynn grinned. "Thanks, but you've had enough mud slung at you for one night because of me. If I end up spending the night in Sankerris…"

"I don't live in Sankerris," Thomas told him. "I live in a half-derelict watchtower on the cliffs near Morvah. It's got a comfortable sofa and all-round views. It's peaceful. You'll be safe for tonight."

"I… Thomas, Robert's not dangerous, you know."

You could've fooled me. Thomas bit it back. If he was, the only person who could find out and have it mean anything useful would be Flynn himself. Probably the hard way. "Whatever you say," he said again quietly. "So, where to, sir? Bunk two, or Zillah Treen's B&B—which I believe has garden gnomes—or…"

Flynn laughed. "The derelict tower sounds good, if you're sure. Thank you."

***

The Land Rover's headlights sturdily probed the night ahead. The creaking, road-rattled silence within it was not awkward, though it had prevailed for the last ten miles. Flynn had left his jacket behind in the pub. Seeing him shiver, Thomas reached to notch up the heater. He wasn't used to finding anyone other than Belle in his way when he made that move, and his wrist brushed Flynn's knee. Neither flinched, and Thomas sat up again, repressing a smile at himself. It was one step off a comedy grab for his knee while changing gear.

And that was not the worst of it. In the cab's increasing warmth, Thomas found himself involuntarily noticing Flynn's scent, which was warm and real beneath his aftershave. He smelled of his life, of the sea, a faint tang of engine oil sometimes prickling through.

Soon they would be home. Thomas wondered why the prospect of having a stranger in his orderly home overnight was not triggering all his alarms. In fact he felt weirdly serene. His knuckles throbbed, showing him a connection, and he smiled.

"That was quite a punch," Flynn suddenly observed, as if reading his thoughts.

"Yeah. Sorry."

"Don't be. Like I say, it was a bit of a work of art. And he had it coming."

"I'm glad you think so."

Another silence fell, briefly this time, fraught with Flynn's tension. Thomas waited. "All that stuff he came out with," Flynn said eventually, "about me, and the flying, and… Aren't you gonna ask?"

Thomas shrugged. The watchtower had appeared on the horizon, its western flank lit by the growing moon. "Assume you'll tell me, when you're ready. Will you get that gate for me?"

Chapter Four
Deeper

Flynn stood in the centre of the round living room. Belle was at his side. Thomas saw him reassessing her size, now that he was seeing her against domestic objects, as he had done himself on first bringing her home, her great shadow rising silently on the watchtower's walls. She liked Flynn, to Thomas's relief. He hadn't yet asked her to accept a visitor, but when he had unlocked the door to let them in, she had come to greet him as she had at the air show, her big head down, stringy tail waving. She was carefully sniffing Flynn over. Flynn looked flattered and nervous in equal measure.

Thomas smiled. "Are you two all right?"

Flynn glanced up. He did look a bit thrown, Thomas thought. More than could be explained by the attentions of Belle. "Yes, fine." He flashed him a smile. "I miss animals, actually. I used to work with sniffer dogs before I started search and rescue." Thomas waited for him to elaborate on this, but his expression became abstracted once more. "God, it's quiet here, isn't it?"

"Mm. Very. Scared the crap out of me at first." Thomas saw him nod, as if in gratitude for the permission to be unnerved. "Can I get you a drink?"

"Please."

"Make yourself comfortable. Have a look around."

There wasn't much to see, but when Thomas emerged from the kitchen, Flynn was wandering around the room with some of the distracted awe he remembered from his own first sight of it. It had felt—not churchlike, but perhaps the way a church would feel to a religious man. He hadn't altered it much, beyond a couple of bright rugs, some whitewash on the walls, and such bookshelves as could be sensibly arranged against a curving surface. A bare space, old flagstones cool underfoot. In the winter, freezing. A small electric tank had been fitted to provide his hot water, and other than that, he had been too numb to care.

He held out the glass he was carrying. An ordinary white wine, though crisp and cold. It had been that, vodka or PG Tips, and on some level he couldn't quite yet understand, Thomas felt he wanted to make a good impression. "Here. Only civilised thing I've got. Do you like the place?"

"Oh. Ta." Flynn took the glass, said suddenly, unguardedly, as if unaware he was voicing the thought, "I love it. I'd move in tomorrow." He blushed to the hairline and ran a hand into his fringe. "Oh God. I can't believe I said that."

I can't believe I'd like to ask you. Thomas let his own surprise become a snort of laughter, which let them both off the hook. "Nor can I, but don't worry. It had a weird effect on me, as well."

"Really? Not *that* weird, I shouldn't think." He shook his head. "Makes me think of—being free, or happy, or…"

He trailed off, but Thomas, wanting to pursue the revelation rather than repress it for their mutual comfort, said quietly, "When does that happen?"

"What—free and happy?" Flynn glanced at him in surprise. "When I was flying, I suppose. Taking one of the Sea Kings up at first light." He swallowed. "Not that I—well, Rob told you. I don't anymore." This time when he fell silent, Thomas could see that a push for more would have hurt him. He nodded, waiting for him to find his way past the moment. His shadowed gaze found the piles of books that had not yet made it onto shelves. Thomas wasn't sure himself why he let them gather dust in piles on the floor, except that their disorder, unlike every other kind, was somehow bearable to him. Flynn said, smiling, "Did you just move in?"

"No. I...I've been here for two years. You're just my first guest." They exchanged a look, in which Flynn acknowledged the honour and Thomas some gratitude at not being taken for some lonely lunatic or serial killer. God, it *had* been two years, and in all that time he had never admitted anyone but electricians and plasterers beyond the vast black-oak door of his fortress. "Is the wine okay?"

Flynn, who appeared to have forgotten about it, lifted his glass. "Yes, great. Where's yours?"

Thomas smiled. He shoved his hands into the pockets of his jeans. "I have an alcohol problem, as so well advertised by Robert Tremaine. It's mostly under control, but...I have my moments. I have to take care. Having said that, I will have one glass with you over a meal, if you're hungry."

Flynn trailed him into the kitchen. It was small, and for the first time Thomas found himself troubled by his visitor's presence. He supposed that when he came out here he was very focused—efficient, getting through the business of feeding himself because he needed to, not because it brought him any pleasure. Flynn's occasional comments, undemanding as they were, unsettled him, distracted him from his efficient assemblage of garlic, onions, chicken fillets. Here too, as in the Rover, he could not get away from his physical reality. Could not turn without his senses flaring to the sight of him, the clean vivid scent…

The second time he dropped his vegetable knife, Flynn shut up and took himself out of Thomas's way, as if sensing the disarray he was causing. He settled in a corner chair by the kitchen table and picked up the newspaper Thomas had left there that morning. Belle's gentle, inquisitive nosing around the room, back and forth between them like some mute messenger, kept their silence from becoming awkward, and Thomas began to relax. By the time he was ready to put down the two fragrant plates on the table, his hands were steady again, and he could find a real smile. "There you go."

"My God. A doctor, *and* he cooks."

Thomas gave this thought. He didn't really think of his meal preparations as cooking. He rotated six or seven basically nutritious recipes, that was all. But when he tried the chicken, it did seem to have a real flavour for once. He smiled at Flynn over the table, and poured him a fresh glass of wine. "Mmm. Highly eligible, apart from those few flaws your mate pointed out. Can't think why I haven't been snapped up."

"Oh, God. I'm so sorry. I dragged you there and…"

"And he's not your responsibility. Neither am I. We don't even have to talk about him."

"Don't we?" Flynn looked as if the possibility of not doing so came as a revelation as well as a relief. "You know, that would be nice. He's been in my face a bit lately." He applied himself to the food for a few moments, then glanced around the kitchen, back into the living room's round cavern beyond it. "Okay. This is very good. I like your dog. I like your…I've already made it painfully clear that I like your house. How did you find it? It doesn't look derelict to me."

Thomas gave him a glimmering look. "Well, you haven't seen upstairs yet. As for how I got it—very cheap, is the answer. There's actually a demolition order on it."

"You're kidding. Isn't it listed?"

"It was. It's one of a chain of towers strung all the way round the north coast. They were used to keep a watch out for smugglers—or by them, to lure ships in with lights, depending on whose legend you listen to. Lots of history. But this one's about ready to crumble into the sea."

Flynn's eyes widened. Thomas noted the expansion of their pupils, and smiled. He looked less fazed than allured by the concept of plunging off the cliff in a welter of masonry. Thomas recalled his own first response to the news of his home's drawback—a stir in his gut, a tug, like gravity, at the idea of life-terminating risk, a vision of the brief sweet avalanche such a conclusion would be—and he wondered at the qualities of a man who would share his moment of excitement. His ultimate indifference. Flynn said softly, "Will it go before we finish dinner, you reckon?"

"Oh, any time over the next century or so, according to the council surveyor. They don't seem in much more of a hurry than that to knock it down, which is useful for me—though I rent it by the month, just in case."

Another easy silence fell. "How's your friend?" Flynn asked suddenly, breaking Thomas's reverie. "The one you were going to help the other week... Victor, was it? In the boathouse?"

"Oh, Victor..." Thomas sighed. He thought about reaching for the Riesling, but Flynn's glass was still full, and somehow the impulse was not as strong as usual anyway. "He's out of the boathouse, at any rate. For now. Vic's a combat-stress case. Army. Three tours in Afghanistan, and he's pretty much destroyed. Drinks too much, can't deal with people. Shuts himself up in his lair every so often. I'm not surprised it looks good to him." He fell silent. It had struck him that, barring a few hard-won disciplines and social graces, he could have been describing himself, and he was suddenly afraid that Flynn had not missed the parallels, either. His expression was extraordinary. Thomas thought he had never seen such compassion—muted, bright-eyed, fierce—in a human face. He felt some dammed-up thing inside him start to strain behind its walls. "He'll be okay," he said roughly. "If the bloody MoD coughs up his compensation, anyway. Are you finished there? Go and sit down and I'll make us some coffee."

Flynn got up. If he minded their conversation's sudden ending, he didn't let it show. "Okay. Thanks for dinner." He put out a hand to scratch behind Belle's ears, and she paced a little way after him as he left the kitchen, then cast an anxious backward glance at Tom and returned to sit at his feet.

Tom was glad that Flynn had obeyed him without question. He needed, fiercely, to be alone for a short time. He had forgotten the pains and joys of serious, significant human interaction—of talking, about something other than the weather, and of being heard. Barely aware of his own actions, he switched the kettle on and turned to start the washing up.

"Thomas?"

He froze. Damn, he should have tried not to let the cutlery clatter. He might have known that Flynn was too polite a guest to leave him to clear up, no matter how much he needed the break. He went through to the living room, wiping soap suds off his hands with a tea towel. Flynn was kneeling between two piles of his uncategorised books, apparently sharing a perusal of them with his wolfhound. "Yes? You okay?"

"Fine. But leave the dishes. I'll do them later."

Thomas looked at him. His presence altered the room in ways Thomas could not account for. Always somehow numinous, now lit by a single lamp in the corner, it had even more of a solemn, waiting air about it, as if any moment it would be filled by the song of angels or mermaids. Well, he could hear the sea, a distant, almost subsonic booming in the cliff-caverns far below.

"It's okay," he said. "I'll just run them through now. It won't take five minutes."

"This is quite a collection," Flynn commented, as if he hadn't heard him. He was carefully turning over the pages of a 1960s account of the Kennedy assassination. Fascinating, practically written on the day. Thomas found himself more interested in the movements his hands made. Capable, deft. Incredibly gentle. Thomas wanted, with a violence that shocked him, to feel their touch on his skin. His mouth dried out. "Henry James, Thackeray, DIY," Flynn continued, glancing over the wildly eclectic mix. "And yet everything else is so organised and…" he gestured to the well-scrubbed flagstone floor, to the room's other surfaces, giving back the lamplight without a trace of dust, "…so beautifully clean."

Thomas swallowed. He never spoke to anyone about his compulsion towards order. Barely acknowledged it to himself. But Flynn wasn't challenging him. His expression was kind, as if he already understood. "I know. I feel as if I have to."

"Like the washing up."

"Yes. I feel as if I have to."

Flynn uncurled from the floor. Not taking his warm gaze from Thomas, he went to the sofa, sat down and stretched one arm along the back of it. Crossed one ankle over his knee. He smiled at Thomas, a long, slow smile that left no room for doubt. "Leave it," he said huskily. "Come here."

So Thomas came to sit beside Flynn. It was awkward—Flynn had not moved his arm, and the sofa was not large, but he thought he had made a reasonably casual job of it until he realised he was still clutching at the tea towel. The bloody undone dishes tugged and nipped at his mind, and he shivered, trying to push the compulsion away. Normally it would not matter; normally he would not miss much by giving in to it. Tonight, however, a handsome green-eyed man was sitting with him in his sea-washed eyrie—one of the loveliest things Thomas had ever clapped eyes on, now he let himself know it—and to turn away his attention seemed criminal.

Then where was he supposed to focus it? The sofa was quite small, but still there had been no need for him to settle within six inches of his guest, in flagrant violation of both their sets of personal space. If he looked down, there were Flynn's lean, powerful thighs, encased in their worn denim. If he looked up—if he tried to meet his eyes—they would be…oh, God, shockingly close, nose to nose, practically, one unthinking inch off a kiss.

He forgot about the dishes. Flynn said, "Look at me," and his reflexive obedience closed the gap.

Another man's mouth under his own. Thomas sucked in an astonished breath and felt Flynn laugh and choke as it was snatched up from his lungs.

"Sorry," Thomas mumbled against Flynn's smile. God, Flynn tasted of sea salt. He was so warm. He reached up and placed a hand on Thomas's shoulder—an open hand, no restraint, just a palm circling his clavicle, tenderly round and round the protuberant bone, even when its fingers closed, no restraint. And so the choice was Thomas's, when the hundred reasons why he shouldn't flickered like sheet-lightning through his mind and he leaned hungrily forward anyway, into Flynn's taste of sunlight and salt, the evanescent sweetness of the Riesling.

He moaned, taking hold of the edge of Flynn's T-shirt. His fingers felt clumsy and damp, but Flynn briefly touched the back of his hand in a gesture of assent and suggestion, his mouth opening under Thomas's, slow as a sea anemone. Instinct stirred in Thomas, and he shyly let his tongue press inward, feeling the welcoming flutter of Flynn's before he could recoil at his own daring.

How long since he had touched human skin not brought to him for diagnosis, healing? How long since he had… Oh God, rhetorical bloody questions. Thomas always knew almost to the minute when he had last had sex. A shudder ran through him. "Flynn… Flynn, no. Stop."

Flynn had closed his eyes, as if in concentration. Now he opened them in concern. "You're pale," he said. "You all right?"

"Yes. No, of course not." Now that his mouth was off Flynn's—an inch off, anyway—all he wanted to do was press it back, restore the kiss that had made his heart ache and race. Which, perversely, now he had decided that this was an impossibility, had called up his erection as hot and strong as could be managed in the confines of his cords. God, he ached. He wanted Flynn, wanted to fuck him, be fucked by him—he didn't much care which. "We can't," he said, his voice unsteady with regret. "You're with someone, and I…I'm screwed up, Flynn, beyond bloody human imagination. Not fit to be with anybody."

Flynn sat in silence for almost a minute, watching him. He reached up the pads of his fingers and ran them over Thomas's brow. Thomas knew that ineradicable marks of pain had gathered there, and hated them. He didn't mind looking older, but not like that. Flynn didn't seem to mind them, though—was targeting them with his caress. "I know," he said, gently. "You've told me—some of it, anyway. And it takes a nutter to know one. You must've gathered that I'm not renowned for sanity myself." He pushed his fingers back from Thomas's temple, into his hair. He smiled. "As for Robert—yeah, you're right. It's a mess, and it's not over. But technically, for tonight at least, he…gave me to you."

Chapter Five
Turning Tide

Thomas spared one moment to glance over at Belle, who had appeared in the doorway. She could be unpredictable when people touched him. "Belle, bed," he ordered her hoarsely, and after giving him one look of benign curiosity, she turned herself around and disappeared into the kitchen's shadows.

He was not sure how he had got here. Could not recall any one moment when he had decided to sit up on the sofa, reach round Flynn to grab the back of it and move to straddle him. It wasn't at all his usual MO. He vaguely remembered being considered a good lover, unless that handful of long-ago acquaintances had been lying to him, and he'd never been afraid to initiate. To shift like this, though, powerful, smooth, and kneel across his lap, the gesture explicit, almost—in Thomas's small experience of the genre—bloody pornographic.

Flynn gasped, pupils expanding with excitement once more, their darkness almost drowning the green. This time when Thomas's hands closed on his T-shirt, he arched his back in an explicit gesture of his own, the muscles down his belly contracting into shapely patterns as he drew his shoulders forward. *Yes. Take it off.* But Thomas was not ready for that yet, wanted badly before he did so to run his hands up under the fabric, to touch without seeing the silk-skinned pectorals, to find with blind precision the nipples he'd felt hardening at his first caress. He closed thumb and finger on them, gently squeezing, and felt Flynn leap like a fish beneath him. A hand on his nape—careful still, but this time brooking no resistance—and Thomas let himself plunge back into the interrupted kiss, capturing Flynn's lower lip between his teeth for one instant in the lightest teasing nip before meeting him, mouth to mouth, tongue to tongue, unrestrained now and dead serious.

Flynn made a sound whose urgency he recognised, and he unlocked one hand from its grip on his shoulder and ran it, slowly, searching, down over his heaving chest and belly, down again. Some part of Thomas wanted to give up and die of the pleasure, the intimacy and companionship, of the kiss, but he had to see. Sitting back, hearing Flynn moan as their contact broke, he looked down. Nice button-fly Levis, tight-fitting and soft with wear, their dirty-denim shade acquired the hard way. Straining across the crotch...

"Oh, God, look at you," Thomas whispered, smiling as Flynn dazedly obeyed, and both watched in ragged-breathed intentness as Thomas slipped the first silver button from its hole, then the next and the next. Black cotton boxers underneath, lifting immediately to the swell of his erection. Their hands tussled briefly over the task of easing back the elastic, pulling those and his jeans down far enough. "Look at you."

Thomas hadn't spent the best part of the week just gone thinking about this man's cock, although he now accepted that he had spent most of it thinking about him. If he had allowed himself such speculation, though, he might have come up with a vision like this. Long, hard, in graceful proportion with the rest of him.

Sharing some of his colours—bronze in the lamplight, indigo veins patterning. At full stretch, Thomas thought, mouth drying out in excitement, but then as he stared rising harder still, the head darkening.

Flynn shuddered beneath him. A glimmer appeared in the opening of his glans, the sensitive meatus, rose and spilled. "Thomas…"

"Yes. What is it?"

"I want to see you. Take your shirt off."

"You do it."

"Oh Christ." Flynn jerked forward, visibly did his best to be polite with the buttons of the nice linen shirt, then gave up and ripped. He shoved the garment off Thomas's shoulders, moaned as Thomas at last grabbed hold of his T-shirt and tore it over his head for him. "Yes," Flynn whispered. "God, look at your beautiful skin."

Helplessly Thomas obeyed him, glancing down, seeing Flynn's beauty—and, yes, astonishingly, his own—by contrasts. Growing up, he had always been as brown as Flynn by this time of the year, and he knew he had marks of desert burning almost branded into him, but otherwise he was pale. He never so much as took off his jacket outside if he could help it, even on the beach—didn't want to be seen.

"Like satin," Flynn told him, and Thomas, leaning to lock them both tight into the next kiss, felt his belt blindly unfastened, his cords unbuttoned, unzipped. Felt his shaft gently seized through the fabric of his briefs. The sound this gesture wrung from him was to his own ears so desperate and carnal that he tried to recoil, but Flynn stilled him with a touch to his shoulder. "No. It's all right. Do what you want."

"You don't even know what I want," Thomas chided him softly, touched to the marrow by his willingness, at the same time almost scared at how soon it had been offered. Now Flynn's caressing hand was reaching down and under to cup his balls. "You don't know… Easy, Flynn. We don't need to go so fast."

"Why not? I do know what you want," Flynn breathed. "Stand up and let me take the rest of your clothes off. Come here and… Oh, you don't know *me*. You can fuck yourself on me till you're bone dry. Till you're drained, and burned out, and you can't feel a thing anymore. I can hold on for you forever. I don't need—I don't even need—"

"Flynn!" Thomas cut him off, appalled. He couldn't escape the insistent pressure being brought to bear between his legs, but he reached and took Flynn's face in his hands. "My God, is that what *you* want?"

Flynn sobbed. Thomas froze in horror. They both did. The sound had come without contortion of Flynn's flushed and eager face, as if someone behind his mask had spoken. A message from a hostage at gunpoint. "No!" he choked out, whether in denial or an answer to his question Thomas couldn't work out. "Oh…Thomas…"

"Tell me. For God's sake, Flynn—talk."

"It's *not* what I sodding well want. But…"

"But what?" Carefully, Thomas pulled away the hand that was still clumsily trying to force the situation on, and Flynn cried out and flung his arms around his neck.

Jesus Christ. "It's all right," Thomas whispered, throat closing in astonishment. His cock ached at the sudden cessation of touch, a brief pang, but then all he could feel was the terrible heat of tears not his own against his cheek. "What is it? What's wrong?"

"Don't. I can't…"

Thomas gave it thought, distractedly but thoroughly holding him. He reckoned that Flynn probably could, if undisturbed by whatever preconceptions about performance and delivery he imagined Thomas had, or memories of what he was used to having to deliver to someone else.

"It's all right," he repeated, an old mantra, worn almost to meaninglessness. Often a lie too. Thomas didn't know. But it was still of service—Flynn relaxed a little. "All right," Thomas murmured against his ear. "You're all right."

He pushed his hand down into the space between their bodies. Flynn was still erect. Awkwardly, but without hesitation, Thomas took hold of him.

Long, slow strokes, easy as sunlight, never relinquishing the embrace. By the tenth or eleventh of them, Flynn was melting, undone. He managed, on a half-choked rasp, "Got to make it good for you too," but Thomas only shook his head, brushing a hot smile against Flynn's neck.

"What's good for me," he whispered, not missing a beat of the inexorable stroking, "is if you come. Just come for me. Come..."

It shouldn't have worked. Little as he knew about him, Thomas was sure that Flynn was used to stronger meat than this. Just to kiss him, and clumsily jerk him off... But Flynn's eyes flew open, and he seized Thomas's shoulders, his cock pulsing hard in his grasp. His climaxing shout was shot through with fear, as if he were trying and failing to ride a wave, plunging towards unimaginable wipeout. He jolted forward. "Thomas, no. It'll tear me apart."

"I'll pick up the bits," Thomas said against his ear, holding him painfully hard. He worked up the beat to a brief, rough frenzy, and felt Flynn convulse in his embrace. Gasped in pleasure and relief as the hot splash hit his wrist and spilled over his hand. "There. There. Come on."

"There'll be nothing—nothing left..."

But there was. Thomas kept tight hold of the remains, while Flynn's cries faded and his respiration climbed back down from assault-course wild to a rhythm that would allow for ragged laughter, and, after an interval, speech. "God almighty. Thomas, I'm sorry. What did you…? What did you do?"

Thomas smiled. A strange thought occurred to him, triggered by who knew what associations in his fractured memory. Intimacy, perhaps. Warm skin against his own. He said, unsteadily, "I used to have friends, you know. They used to call me Tom."

"Oh." Flynn shivered with an aftershock, and said the name softly, just a movement of his lips on Thomas's skin. *Yes,* Thomas thought. *That was who I was to everyone—to myself, even—before I joined up, before Captain Thomas Penrose got himself born.* "Tom," Flynn repeated, and Tom let his eyes close, burying his face in Flynn's hair.

An interval passed. Gradually the room fell again into its accustomed sea-whisper silence. Flynn sat curled in Tom's arms, or perhaps it was the other way round—it was hard to tell from their tangle. Either way, Tom was still hard, his erection pressing warmly to Flynn's thigh. It seemed to him a distant concern. For the moment it felt to him as if seeing and feeling Flynn come— crashing whatever barricades that had involved—had been enough. Then embarrassment stirred, and he tried to shift back a little.

"Hoi," Flynn whispered hoarsely. "Where are you off to?"

"Nowhere. Just… Not everyone likes to be prodded after…"

"After?" Flynn interrupted him, easing away far enough for Tom to see his puzzled, frowning smile. "Do you somehow think we're done here?"

"Well, I know things aren't simple for you." Not even the animal reflex of orgasm, Tom thought. The simplest thing in the world, snarled up inside you till it looked less like pleasure than pain. "We *can* be done, if you like."

Flynn shook his head. His breath was still unsteady, a damp flush painting his cheeks. "You're a one-off, aren't you?" he said, running a hand over Tom's hair. "That's a first for me, at any rate. Look, if you haven't got any plans for all that potential, I do, and…" He paused, raising glowing eyes to Tom's. "Something was said about an upstairs."

Their hand-in-hand ascent of the watchtower's stairs should have been awkward, a comedy. But Flynn put out a hand and led him, negotiating the steep curve backwards, smiling down on him, and his presence made a small ritual, a circle dance, of the climb. Tom felt as if he could see them from outside, as if he was the tower, watching them. *Shadow puppets on a wall.* Shaking his head, he tried to restore a sense of reality. A tumble on the sofa was one thing—he didn't recall one second when he felt he'd had a choice. But taking Flynn to bed…

They stood together in the round upper chamber. Flynn, who had not let go of his hand, surveyed its moonlit circle. "Beautiful," he said, then turned to look straight at Tom and repeated it—*beautiful*—on such a note that Tom thought few human creatures must ever have heard, let alone one man from another. Let alone him.

He felt his joints try to slacken, his cock grow taut and hard, trying to lift to his belly in the confines of his pants. Taking Flynn to bed was the only thing in the wide wild world to do, and if it damned him, did nothing but remind him of his losses, so be it. Flynn had led him up the stairs, but it was Tom who kissed him, said, "Come on," and pulled him down after him onto the bed.

When matters became urgent—which they soon did; Tom could hold his fire for a more than respectable time but was entirely male and human—he murmured a laughter-shaken *wait a second* against Flynn's mouth and rolled out from under him. In the bathroom, he knew a moment's near panic, then took a breath and pulled out a box at the back of the cabinet's bottom drawer. The lubricant was near to hand, from the rare nights when he needed to jerk off and his own dry touch was unpleasing to him. But he hadn't, for God's sake, always lived like a sodding monk, had he? No, there, right at the back, and just within their sell-by date...

When he returned from the bathroom, Flynn was watching. He had taken the opportunity to skin out of his clothes and array himself on Tom's bedspread, flat on his stomach, propped on his elbows. He had the air of a man who knew from long experience that the inviting pose would work. Tom, freezing to a halt at the foot of the bed, tried not to let it. Whatever sexual routine Flynn employed—whatever had made him astonished, that Tom could give without immediately needing to grab back—he didn't want to fall in with it. But Flynn's gaze had settled on him, front, down and centre, and he supposed his persistent erection, his hypnotised stare, hardly conveyed a refusal. "God, Flynn..."

"Yes. Come here," Flynn said, then paused, as if to judge his next words carefully. As if gauging him. "Get your clothes off. And come and shove that in me before it explodes."

The crudity was deliberate. Delicate somehow too. Tom knew that, by the standards of soldiers and Navy men, his own language was restrained—comically so, according to those with whom he'd shared barracks and field-hospital surgeries. He didn't consider himself more than ordinarily decent—just shy of rough words out of context or for their own sakes. Flynn's context was new to him. Flynn, who looked as if he possessed a bone-deep decency of his own, could stir him profoundly with a well-judged obscenity or two. Tap a vein of raw sexuality he wasn't sure he could bear to confront.

"Tom, come *here*."

Tom fell on him. He tried not to—not in the sense of a lion falling on a bloody antelope, but knew he hadn't been much gentler. He pushed him down onto his belly, feeling the sense of fit, of blessed homecoming, as his cock slid up between strong male thighs. Panting, bracing to one arm, he reached for the box of condoms, and felt Flynn suddenly close one hand on his wrist.

"Don't bother. I'll take the lube—you're a big lad, Dr. Tom, in case nobody's told you—but…I trust you."

Good luck with the novel fucking ways he comes up with of committing suicide every other week…

Tom took hold of his shoulders. With the exception of his mother's, Rob Tremaine's was the last voice he wanted to hear in his head at this moment. "Flynn. Don't be soft. You shouldn't trust any man, not like that."

"Any?" Flynn, glancing back at him wide-eyed, tried for a weak grin. "How often do you think I—"

"I don't care how often. I'm not a saint, and even if I had been, I'm a doctor. I do a shift in Penzance casualty every week— I'm exposed to blood all the time. I get myself checked, but, Flynn…"

"All right, all right," Flynn capitulated. For a second, Tom thought there were tears in his eyes. Of frustration? Maybe. If it was Tremaine he was getting compared to, he had no doubt that Flynn could launch him like a cruise missile, no questions asked.

Tom flashed back helplessly to that vulpine grin, raw-boned build. Yes, Rob would have ploughed his way up Flynn so hard the poor bastard would be tasting his come by now. Tom wondered if any other approach seemed tame to Flynn by comparison—if Rob expanded to fill his horizon, blocking the light…

"Tom, for God's sake. What are you waiting for? Come here. Let me do the honours."

Tom struggled back into the moment. Flynn's deft attentions with condoms and lubricant kept him there, breathing deeply for control, but as soon as the practicalities had been seen to and Flynn had stretched out on his stomach, doubts assailed Tom once more. Yes. Eclipsed. Flynn had said he was big, but maybe it wasn't enough. Safely sheathed and drenched in lube, straining at Flynn's entrance, Tom slipped a hand beneath him. Said, as gently as he could, "You're not hard."

Flynn shivered. He rubbed his forehead on his folded arms. "Are you...are you surprised, after the wring-out you gave me before? I will be, once you're inside me. Come on. Please."

Carefully Tom explored his softened shaft. He uncapped the lubricant once more and eased back, sliding two fingers down between his buttocks. Finding and circling his hole. He heard Flynn suck a breath. "That okay?"

"Mm. God, yes. Better than." Flynn moaned, arched his back. Drew his legs up to accommodate the touch, and Tom pushed the caress forward, slipping one slick fingertip inside, exerting gentle pressure just inside the rim. "Yes. Don't stop that. I'm just... I'll be better in a minute." Suddenly he lifted his head and glanced back at Tom over his shoulder, his smile nervous, hard to read. "You're different, you know. When you touch me, when you look at me...you make the world seem different. Less of a battlefield."

Tom didn't know what to say. His throat was closing. "Good," he whispered, for want of anything better, and brought a second fingertip to bear, gingerly stretching.

Flynn jumped. It was a tiny movement, repressed a fraction of a second too late. Tom read it instantly—pain, too sharp to hide. Immediately, involuntarily, his touch became medical. "Flynn, for God's sake. You're hurt down here. You're swollen." Not waiting for Flynn to move or speak, he sat up, reached over him and switched on the bedside light. "Let me see."

"Tom… What the fuck?" Flynn scrambled backward, raising a hand to shield his eyes. The light was stark. Tom read away insomniac nights here, propped against the headboard where Flynn was now hopelessly trying to retreat. Trying, at the same time, to pull up a sheet, because both of them knew that Tom, who had picked up a tiny swell of muscle in the dark, was not about to miss the bruises with which he was painted from stomach to groin. Couldn't pretend to, even if he wanted. "Shit," Flynn groaned, drawing his knees up to his chest. "Couldn't you have just left well alone?"

Tom would have liked to. Shock was taking care of his erection, but the sudden shut-off from an arousal so massive and sweet was sending nausea through him, and a cold dull ache. "Sure," he said unsteadily, coming to kneel beside Flynn. He tugged off the condom, abruptly sickened by it. "If anything had been well, I'd have left it. Jesus, Flynn." He ran a bewildered hand into his hair. "If you're in an abusive relationship, there's people who can help you. I'll help you."

Flynn broke into laughter. It was the first unpleasant sound that Tom had heard from him—bitter, full of pain. "Who the fuck are you—Oprah bloody Winfrey?" He seized a corner of the rumpled bedspread and pulled it over his thighs, as if his own lax cock suddenly shamed him. "The Navy deals with that kind of shit in-house, I promise. And if I am—which I'm not—you'd better believe, it goes two ways. I'm not a hurt lamb, Tom. I ask for it. I fucking beg."

Tom sat back on his heels. He transfixed Flynn on one dark look. "Well," he said stonily. "The difference with me, sunbeam, is that you're not gonna get it."

He dragged out blankets from the linen basket, a cotton sheet. Picked up a pillow from the bed and did not quite throw it at him. Flynn, not meeting his eyes, took the things from him and made for the stairs. Tom turned his back on him.

He got almost as far as the bed before his brow contracted, and he turned and padded silently to the third stair down, where he could watch without being seen. He knew how cold the stone flags were to bare feet. Naked, he crouched, wrapping his arms round his knees. He saw Flynn stumble over to the sofa and lie down, curling himself up in the blanket. He saw Belle pad cautiously across the living room towards him and stand apprehensively for almost a minute before jumping up beside him. Flynn started violently and made a sound that accurately reflected the shock of having a dog the size of a small pony leap on him out of the dark, but Belle laid herself placidly down beside him, and after a moment, he buried his face in her coat. Tom got up, stiff and cold to the bone, and went back to the rumpled bed.

***

Tom had adopted Belle just before he moved into the watchtower. He had never known the place without her, and its unbreathing silence, as he made his way downstairs in the dawn light, sent a chill through him. The pillow, shaken out, was placed neatly on the sofa, the sheet folded on top. The dinner dishes from last night had been washed and were gleaming in the rack.

Flynn was sitting outside on one of the rocks that dotted the narrow strip of turf that divided the tower's foot from the cliff. He had both blankets wrapped around his shoulders. Tom wondered how long he had been there. Belle, if not exactly leaning on him, was sitting close enough to shed some body warmth and had an air of being on guard. When she heard the back door open, she got up and came over to greet Tom, waving her long tail, but then circled straight back to Flynn. *Looking after him, aren't you? You're a better host than I was.*

He said his name gently, and Flynn turned around. For a moment his face was a blank, his eyes as empty as the grey sea horizon on which they had been fixed. Then he smiled, far more warmly than Tom thought he deserved. Real, Tom asked himself, or a reflex of self-defence? After last night he couldn't be sure. "Morning."

"Morning," Tom said, taking up a diffident position on the rock beside him. "Here. Made you a cup of tea. Wasn't sure how you took it, but…"

"But you'll have observed that, although I am clearly fit and trim, I have my weaknesses, and I enjoy my food. You therefore made it nice and strong, with milk and sugar, which is exactly right. You're a perceptive man." Their eyes met in wry acknowledgement of what his acuity had cost them both last night.

"Listen," Flynn continued after an interval, gratefully wrapping cold fingers round the mug. "Some of that bruising is from the other week. That wave knocked the holy crap out of me. And I've done a rescue since, a tough one. Some of it's from then."

"Not… Not all, though."

"No. Not all." They sat for a while in silence, and once more somehow it was not uncomfortable. Despite everything. A rosy May dawn was trying to get itself born through the mists on the moors to the east, every moment the air was soaking up more and more light. Flynn said, beginning a smile that promised to be brighter still, "That was some great sex we nearly had, wasn't it?"

Tom snorted. He shifted his backside closer to Flynn's and put an arm around him. "Yeah. The best."

"What I wouldn't give for another crack…"

Tom said nothing, but tried to indicate by his posture that the world was very wide, and Flynn a free agent within it. That he, Tom, was both available and open to suggestion. Flynn sighed and leaned lightly into him, as if seeking his warmth. "Oh God. You don't understand."

"Ready to tell me," Tom said, not as a question. "Come on."

"Rob was my copilot," Flynn began. That much told, he paused, but Tom didn't need him to elaborate on the significance. He had seen the bond in action, over and over again. It instantly threw new light on Tremaine—promoted him from dangerous nuisance to Flynn's brother-in-arms. He nodded, and Flynn went on, with an odd little flicker of gratitude at having been so understood. "Not on search and rescue. We used to do maritime security over at Portsmouth."

"Drugs and weaponry?"

"Yeah. I was good at it, believe it or not. Lieutenant Commander, Airborne Surveillance and Control. I had a six-man team, and…I had Rob." He shivered, shook his head. "Or Rob had me. I'm not sure which. He was always a bit of a force of nature, Tom, but back then I didn't mind so much. We started practically the first night after we'd flown together. You're high as a kite after a risky op, you know? And it doesn't feel like anyone can bring you down except…"

He faded out. Tom gave him a break, from his own attention and the painful narrative, reaching round behind him to pull up the blanket which had started to slip off his shoulder. He finished for him, after a moment, "Except someone who was out there too."

"Yes. Yes, exactly. Happened every time. For him I think it became like a *ritual*, something he had to do, and as soon as I felt that, it—well, it wasn't good anymore. A couple of times—I should've busted him in the chops after the first one—I said no, and either he wasn't listening or he didn't take me seriously, but… God, Tom." Flynn turned a little to look at him. "Why didn't I stop him? I'm not soft, and I'm not anybody's patsy. I…"

"He *is* a force of nature," Tom interrupted him gently. Maybe the question had been rhetorical, but Tom's years as soldier and doctor had showed him a lot of men, a lot of jungle paths. "I know you're a proper hard-arse, Flynn, but blokes like that, once they get into the habit, I think it's like trying to stop a bloody hurricane. And I've known a fair number of pilots. Seconds too. They'd go a long way, do pretty much anything, to protect their bond."

"Is that what I was doing?" Flynn whispered, lifting his hands to his mouth. "Maybe. God, when I listen to you, it doesn't sound so bloody pathetic, but…" He took his hands down, and Tom sensed in the movement of his shoulders his effort to brace and go on. "Anyway. I didn't have much more time to worry about it. Our next callout, my helicopter ditched. She was a Lynx, brand new, top of the range. I got one warning light on the board, and—thirty seconds later she was down."

Down. Tom released a breath. He had seen how they went, these unlikely contraptions of blade and spin, had watched one hit by a missile over a compound in Helmand. A plane, structurally aerodynamic anyway, would sail on briefly, but the birds just dropped when their rotors stopped, pitched down in a screaming flail of metal and howling engines. "Thirty seconds? Did anyone have time to bail?"

"No. I don't remember it, not even hitting the water. I was out cold. All I know about it is what Rob's told me—he was thrown clear. Fuck knows how, but I wouldn't be here otherwise. She wallowed for a minute. Air pocket in the cockpit. Rob shot the glass out, pulled me free. He risked everything to get me,

Tom. When they start to haul under, they suck everything round them down too. I don't know how he did it. I don't know…"

Nor did Tom. He couldn't imagine the superhuman effort it would take for a shocked air-crash victim, dumped unprepared into dark waters, to fight his way back in time to make the save. But weird things happened in combat, in the throes of frightened love. Miracles, if you looked at things that way, and God knew Flynn's presence now, a warm, breathing life in the curve of his arm, seemed pretty much a marvel. It wasn't the time to question Rob Tremaine's heroism, and Flynn wasn't finished—Tom sensed the rest of the story building up in the tensions of his shoulders. He knew what it was. To help him end it, he said, very softly, "All right. What about the others? Your crew?"

"They were in the cabin. It flooded straightaway. They drowned. I lost them all."

Yes, Tom had known. But shock still rocked him. It convulsively tightened his grip on Flynn's shoulders, and he laid a hand to the back of his neck as he lowered his head, curling up. "Oh, fuck, Flynn. Oh, no."

***

"So it was just us two." Long minutes had passed, of intense sea-whisper silence. Flynn had one hand on Belle's collar, the dog having made her way to his distress like some kind of hairy emergency service, the way she always did to Tom on his dark days. His other hand was held in Tom's, bone-crackingly hard. When he had raised his head, his eyes were empty, his voice hollow and calm. "Me and Rob. The enquiry found pilot error. They couldn't check the wreckage—we were out too deep for salvage—and even if there'd been a fault, it still would've been mine. I made all my checks. I thought she was clean. But she was my bird, my ship, and I just wish…I just wish Rob had let me die with her."

Thank God he didn't. Tom wouldn't have said it aloud. It would have been facile, and even if somehow in the course of their brief acquaintance Flynn had become so bright and clear a presence in his life that Tom would have meant it, he didn't expect Flynn to have found any such corresponding comfort in him. He pressed a rough kiss to his temple, and it was as if Flynn had heard the repressed grateful prayer.

"You don't know what it was like," he said roughly. "I was in hospital for weeks, fucking comatose, and—when I woke up, I had every single one of those men's wives, partners, families at my bedside, trying to absolve me, tell me I wasn't to blame, or if I was, they—forgave me."

"Jesus, Flynn."

He released Belle but retained his grip on Tom's hand, wiped a palm across his eyes. "And when they went home, there was just Rob. Day in, day out. I sound like I'm complaining, don't I?"

"No. No, just telling me. Did he help?"

"You have no idea. He just took me over. He hired me a shit-hot Navy lawyer, challenged the enquiry on grounds of lack of evidence. Overturned them too, so instead of being out on my arse I was given retraining and a non-piloting role down here with SAR." He paused, brief laughter shaking him. "Couldn't have got me much further out of the way, unless they'd sent me to Orkney, but I was bloody grateful for the gig. Not that I got here before I'd chucked a spectacular nervous collapse. Psychiatrists, specialist clinics, the lot. Rob paid for it all."

"Didn't the service do anything for you?"

Flynn shrugged. "I saw a couple of Navy shrinks. Got short shrift from them, though. I think I was meant to accept my dishonourable discharge and clear out. I'd taken six of their best down with me, hadn't I?"

Tom nodded bitterly, thinking of Victor. The forces looked after their own, until certain harsh and deep-carved lines of perceived honour or courage were crossed. In Helmand, he'd been expected to kick arse as much as offer counsel to the troubled soldiers who found their way into his office. "Okay. Yes, I can imagine. But—lawyers, that kind of care… It must have cost Robert a fortune."

"Several. I was out of commission for months. His family's loaded, but I know he paid for a lot of it himself. And it wasn't just that, Tom—he transferred down to Hawke to be with me, got a post with SAR. All right, he's possessive, but…if you think about it, that's fair enough. He pretty much owns me."

Bollocks. Tom bit that back too. If that was Robert's line, he could see how Flynn had come to be caught on it. He settled for a gentle, "Nobody owns you, Flynn," rubbing one thumb across the back of his tight-clenched hand.

"I know. I'm sorry. I'm still fucked up, I suppose—I don't always see things right. Either way, he deserves better than he gets from me. I mess with his head at least as much as he does mine. He hates my surfboard, hates my stupid little sports car. I drive him crazy by volunteering for the rescue winch in storms. Like he said, my hundred different ways of committing suicide. He feels like I'm always at the end of my leash, pulling to be away."

"And…are you?"

"Yes. But not the way he thinks. I'd pull away from it all if I could work out how."

Flynn turned his face to Tom's shoulder. After a moment in which his heart and chest ached so much that he couldn't move, Tom closed both arms around him. He didn't know what to say— knew anyway, from bitter experience, the point at which words failed. He kissed the top of Flynn's head, pulled the blankets up tight round him, and wondered after a while if the telling of this story had worn the poor bastard back to sleep, he was so still and silent in his arms.

Then, suddenly, Flynn sat up. He put both hands to Tom's shoulders and eased him back, just far enough to see him properly. To Tom's astonishment, his face was alight with compassion. "You think I'm lost in this, don't you?" he whispered, brushing a fingertip touch to Tom's brow, his lips, the corners of his eyes. "You think I don't see anything else. But I do. You've learned about my kind of pain the hard way. I can see…" Soft, searching kisses followed the touch. Tom shuddered, almost unable to bear them. They targeted every mark that grief had carved into him, and he had thought his own story safely buried far away, subsumed in the better, easier business of dealing with Flynn's. He should have known, shouldn't he, that such a man would not tolerate the one-sided world Tom had built to contain himself. "I can see your cairn," Flynn said, nodding towards the mound of glimmering quartz stones on the turf a few yards away. "Who's it for?"

"David," Tom told him, shocked into truth. "David Reay. He was my assistant medical officer in Helmand. We did three tours together."

"Your lover?"

"Once. He always wanted it, but I couldn't face being gay, not in the army, not out there. Then I realised how stupid that was, and we had one night. He was so bloody happy. Next day he went out with a convoy, to help at the hospital in Lashkar Gar. They were ambushed. He never came back."

Flynn reached for him. Tom thought it was only in comfort. Looking into Flynn's eyes, he saw that was all he intended—the touch that would bridge the gap when words failed, a hand to his shoulder and the side of his face. Tom could hardly bear the kindness of it. The understanding, the compassion—too much, and suddenly, when Flynn's grip tightened, not what he wanted anymore. He gasped. Need seared through him, everything he'd put on hold last night and during the chained-up years just gone. "Flynn…"

"What is it?"

No need to explain. Tom saw the same change transfiguring him. Grief flashing off into hunger, like oil on water catching fire. If they'd had the chance—if life had bound them together, given them some years, was this how they would have solved all their pains? Their joys too, triumphs and disasters, all finding solace or celebration in bed, or out on the flower-starred turf? "That second crack you wanted," he rasped, and waited until Flynn's attention was on him so keenly he felt it like a burn. "For God's sake grab it now."

They crashed down from the rock onto the grass. Flynn's blanket tore loose from his shoulders and Tom caught him, grunting in winded pleasure as his weight impacted, warm and sweet and naked as the day. "Flynn. You'll catch your death."

"Don't care. Just love me. Have me. Do it."

Tom groaned. He snatched the kiss Flynn was fiercely offering and struggled on top, mindful of his lover's bruises, but only just. Flynn resisted briefly then rolled luxuriantly under, stretching out in an ecstasy of surrender. Joyfully he grabbed Tom's pyjama bottoms, dragged them down around his hips and opened his thighs for him. "Come on! Come here!"

Tom stared down in a mix of lust and concern at the tanned, bare flesh on the wet turf. "Oh, I don't want to hurt you."

"Damn you. Get on with it."

Shuddering, Tom obeyed. Spine dissolving in heat, he let his rigid cock shove hard between Flynn's thighs. *Once and once only,* he told himself. *A first time and a last with this perfect and forbidden man.* He thought of David, whose funeral he had not attended, whose name had never passed his lips in three dry-mouthed years, and he reached for Flynn, a gift given him for the night. They were into extra time now, the sun piercing clouds, kissing his bare back with the first real heat of summer—*injury time*, Tom thought, thrusting hard, taking his weight on his arms to spare those bruises, which looked to him like fist marks, not wave tumble or harness. He wouldn't question Flynn's devotion—or thraldom—to Robert Tremaine. He would let him go.

Flynn's hands closed round his backside. His lovely face contorted to a mask lovelier still, the beginnings of orgasm, calling up Tom's own like thunder from the place where he had boxed it up the night before. He noticed irrelevantly that the thyme was flowering, dust-pink blossoms giving off an aromatic tang under the crush of their bodies. Milkwort too, tiny flashes of heaven-blue. Soon all the headlands would be starred with them.

He groaned and stiffened, and Flynn in his extremity surged up beneath him, knocking him down onto his back. Tom yelled inarticulately, heaving up against his weight, feeling his own strength as almost inhuman, this close to the peak. Flynn snarled his name, face contorting, and slammed him back down so hard that the turf abraded skin off him. His shaft was trapped and starting to erupt against Tom's belly. Clenching his fingers in the short hair at his nape, Tom let go and climaxed incandescently, morning sunlight tearing into bloodstained silver fragments in his eyes.

They rolled and tangled halfway to the bloody cliff's edge before they had wrung the coming out of one another. Tom was glad, folding bonelessly down into his lover's arms, that their nearest land-based observer would have to have been in New York.

Chapter Six
Undertow

They managed, somehow, a peaceful and prosaic breakfast. Tom sent Flynn up to shower the grass stains off while he made toast and tea. He had seen the idea of sharing the shower glitter in Flynn's eyes, but it would have been a step too far, brought their one shared night tumbling into this day. It was Sunday, and Flynn due on a long shift at Hawke. Tom would run him up there, and that would be it.

He had told Flynn to help himself from his wardrobe. Flynn's T-shirt from last night was sweat-damped and crumpled beyond redemption, and had been beer-stained even before its ordeal. He looked nice in one of Tom's many identical plain grey Ts. He looked nice, Tom thought, sitting opposite him at his breakfast table. He topped up Flynn's mug from the pot, squaring his shoulders. "Do you... Do you think you'll stay in Cornwall, then?"

Flynn smiled. "Yes," he said, taking his cue. This was their first official polite conversation, Tom's effort, despite their wild night, to send them on their separate ways as friends. "It was just a posting, at first. Everywhere looked the same for a while, you know?" Tom nodded, cradling his mug between his palms—he did. "But I can't imagine being anywhere else now. The surf, and the cliffs, and…at the risk of sounding like a complete hippie, the standing stones. When I saw my first one, I nearly crashed the car. Sat and stared at it for hours."

"They're quite something. Do you remember which one it was?"

"The quoit. The one any blundering tourist can find, right by the road. Lanyon, is it?"

"Yes. Lanyon. That's Belle's favourite too—I take her there every other day for a run."

Flynn looked up from his toast. He absently sucked marmalade from one finger in a gesture which almost wiped Tom's good intentions to oblivion. Their eyes met. *Lanyon Quoit.* Damaged, randomly put back together. None the less lovely for that. Not a promise. Not even a breath of suggestion. Just a place that they both knew.

A faint, strange sound began to filter through their silence. Tom frowned. He knew most of his home's noises by this time, and this was new to him. It sounded like a wasp caught in a jam jar. It seemed to be coming from near the front door where Belle was sitting, her back to the room. Tom got to his feet and went over to her. Unusually, she didn't respond to his voice or his caress, and he saw, with a mix of alarm and amusement, that she had rucked up her normally placid and dignified face into a kind of gargoyle's mask. As he crouched by her, it got worse. She kept her gaze fixed on the door, and slowly, as if having trouble remembering how, she wrinkled her long snout and drew back her lips to reveal both rows of white wolfhound teeth. Belatedly Tom realised that the tiny, high-pitched sound was coming from her. "My God, Belle," he enquired, voice fracturing with laughter. "Is that your *snarl?*"

She looked at him once, reprovingly, then fixed her attention front-centre once more. Thinking he should probably do the same, Tom went to the tower's south window and looked out. He rested his hands on the broad white sill and let go a sigh. "Black Bull Mercedes pickup truck," he said resignedly. "Huge, top of the range, silver trim."

Flynn dropped his face into his hands. "Oh *fuck*."

The truck had been at the far gate when Tom saw it, and God only knew how much farther away when Belle's mysterious alarm system had been triggered. Now it was rolling slowly over the turf track, a growing black monster. Tom and Flynn stood in the watchtower's open doorway, at painful standoff. "Tom, please," Flynn said for the third time. "Just let me walk down and meet him. It'll be fine."

Tom knew he had to say something. Just holding Flynn back by the waist of his jeans was not enough. It wasn't easy. His throat felt full of grit, all his calm acceptance of the situation evaporated in the reality of having to let him go. "This is my home," he managed at length. "It was incredibly hard for me to find one. I'm not ashamed of having had you here, and I'm not about to bloody hide." He turned to him. "Flynn, do this for me. Go inside and take Belle with you. Just for a minute."

He stood out on the sun-blown turf, hands in his pockets. He was astonished and touched by Flynn's compliance, which had been given with set-muscled, gritted-teeth reluctance, and an expression nearly as frightening as Belle's. The thought of it distracted Tom as the vast Mercedes Bull lumbered over the last few yards between them.

He had no idea what he was going to do or say to Rob Tremaine, and he wasn't getting any advance cues. Typically, the truck's windshields were one-way black, giving him only a view of his own insignificant stance against the backdrop of endless moors. Huge metal roll bars, as if the damn thing would ever tip up. Waist-high tractor tyres, a rack of searchlights, the whole thing wrapped up in glossy brand-new metal and shimmering chrome. Might as well have had a deer roped to the grille. Tom could not understand what anyone not towing horses every day could possibly want with such a vehicle. In the narrow Penwith single lanes, they took up a lane and a half.

He stood up straighter, lifting his chin.

An anomaly which had been tugging at his mind since dawn abruptly surfaced. Tom had a fair idea what those brutes cost. What good psychiatry cost too. Rob's family was wealthy, Flynn had said—the branch that had left to make money in London, and apparently succeeded.

Except that Tom was more or less certain they were not. He was pretty sure that Lizzie Tremaine and the string of random men who fathered her children were still living in borderline poverty on the Bay estate. It was the one bloody thing that Tom disliked about Cornwall, and fought with increasing futility to rectify—the gap between rich and poor, the pattern by which more and more homes were sold off for holiday cottages while the estates became ghettoes, hidden from visitors' eyes. Well, it looked as if Rob had found his own solution. More power to him, Tom supposed, watching the truck door swing portentously open.

Suddenly there was warmth at his shoulder, and he realised with a sinking gut that Flynn's cooperation had worn off. At least he'd left the dog indoors.

Rob Tremaine jumped down onto the turf. He looked smaller this morning—possibly only in contrast with his own vast vehicle, but he was holding his hands out in front of him too, angled, palms down. He was cleanly and quietly dressed, and had tamed his red hair back into a neat ponytail. "My God," he said, approaching Tom and Flynn, looking from one to the other. "I do not even know where to *begin* apologising."

***

There was still some tea in the pot. Tom gave it to Tremaine graciously enough, while he sat on the sofa—in the exact spot, Tom thought with a shudder and a sense of disbelief, where he had stroked Flynn to orgasm barely twelve hours before—and explained, big disarming grin flashing, how he had had a rough few days and hit the cider. Not that that was any excuse for his behaviour, which although he didn't remember most of it, had been described to him in lurid detail by his mates, and he gathered he deserved the shiner Tom had left him by way of souvenir. He had said some appalling things. He was grateful to Tom for looking after Flynn, and had come out to collect him to save Tom the trip. They were due on duty in an hour's time.

Flynn had remained silent, perched on the arm of the sofa. His hand was on Belle's head, whether for companionship or to calm her Tom didn't know. She had stopped her weird singing and was now only pulling ever more fantastic and anguished faces at the new arrival. "All right," Flynn said now. "Thank you. Go on. I'll be out in a minute."

Tom tried to flash him a warning look. *No point, Flynn. Just go.* He saw Rob's eyes darken, his smile become fixed. For a moment Tom thought, with a pang of revulsion, that he was going to have to tackle this mess in his own hard-won and thus far inviolate home, but then Robert got to his feet and left, Belle watching his every step.

As soon as he was gone, Flynn came over to him, knelt in front of the room's one armchair, on the edge of which Tom had conducted this second-worst social occasion of his life, took hold of his face with tenderly passionate hands and kissed him. "I'm sorry. So sorry. I shouldn't have let last night happen."

"Do you regret it?"

Flynn's eyes widened. "Christ, no."

"Then forget about it." Tom regretfully traced the lines of his face with gentle fingertips. "What, do you think I'm going to make your life hard over this? Turn up threatening suicide outside your barrack door?" He paused, trying to think of something that would lessen the pain in his eyes. "Get into a deliberate crisis at sea? Would you do that to me?"

Flynn smiled reluctantly. "I might turn up outside *your* barrack door."

"Don't. Go home. Go and sort things out with Rob. If ever things are any different… Well, you know where my barrack is."

***

He was gone, and Tom was alone in his cliff-top solitude, surrounded by the cool light and the whispering silences he had come out here to find, by the four-foot-thick walls in which he had attained some semblance of healing. Which he told himself he needed, and still loved. Where he had plenty of rational ways of filling in a Sunday, none of which involved the crates beneath the stairs. He could sort out his bed linen, for one thing, and the breakfast dishes were untouched. Add in to that the subtle marks of another man's presence all over his house—the soap left in the wrong place, maybe (not that he would look) a bronze-blond hair on a pillow—and, really, his OCD could run rampant in such a way as to leave his incipient alcoholism without a look-in. He might even begin to sort out his books, which were his last bastion against empty days.

He'd start with the dishes. Leaning to pick up Rob's teacup from beside the sofa, he saw on its arm a large, alien and expensive black wallet. He stood up and released a breath. "Oh for fuck's sake." Come to think about it, the fading sound of the pickup's engine had stopped. And Belle was at the door again.

He took the cup to the sink. Then he placed the wallet on the kitchen table, front and centre, in plain sight. He sat down quietly on a chair beside it. He said, "Belle, open the door."

It was normally one of her favourite tricks, but she plainly could not believe being asked to do it now. Nevertheless, after an incredulous look at her defaulting pack leader, she rose up on her haunches, lifted the latch with her nose and, when the wind pushed the door inward far enough, put a paw into the gap and drew it open. "That's a good girl. Now come here."

Tremaine looked disconcerted to find the enemy lair wide open. As if he could not decide whether Tom, waiting at the kitchen table, or the vast dog at his side were least impressed with him. Nevertheless he came to stand in front of them, rage twisting his face. "I'm warning you, Penrose. Leave Flynn alone."

Tom said, "I think you left something. Take it and go."

Tremaine reached his hand out for the wallet. It had been an obvious trick, and he looked humiliated by it now. Tom could feel his own contempt crackling in the air between them like ozone. Suddenly Tremaine banged his fists down on the table's surface. "You're not listening!" he spat. "You think you know who I am, don't you? I promise you, you've got no fucking idea. You go near him again, or I catch him with you, you'll bloody find out." He snatched up the wallet.

Tom, who had barely managed to restrain Belle's defensive lurch, watched in silence, holding her, as he stalked away.

The one thing, Tom thought, which could have made the morning worse was half an inch more of Flynn's discarded T-shirt protruding from behind the sofa cushion. As it was, he couldn't quite work out how Tremaine had missed it. He pulled the garment out. He didn't like dirty things or stale human smells. Normally it would have been a fingertip extraction and straight into the wash.

He took it over to the south window and hitched himself up into its deep alcove. Once curled up there, he gently unfolded the T-shirt between his hands. Raised it to his face and inhaled deeply.

Belle trotted over to the window and gazed up at him. She looked so sorrowful he almost laughed. "Don't be stupid, dog. Just give me a minute. I'll be fine."

***

All the following week, events seemed to conspire to help Tom to chase thoughts of Flynn from his mind. Staff shortages sent him down to the Penzance hospital twice instead of once for his casualty stint, and Victor Travers' compensation case went to court, meaning Tom had to leave Belle with Mrs. Vic overnight while he accompanied his old comrade to London. It was a voluntary task—Victor had a good lawyer, and Tom had only been asked to provide written evidence—but Florence had begged him to provide an escort, certain that her troubled husband would not get there without one. The hearing was much shorter than Tom had expected, and strikingly more successful—someone up the line had had a change of heart, and suddenly Sergeant Travers, instead of being an embarrassing drain on army resources, was a war vet, an honoured soldier in possession of a decent income for wife and family, with enough left over to get the private medical treatment he required.

The difference in Vic was extraordinary. Tom had sat with a pale, mute zombie on the train all the way from Penzance to

Paddington, but on the way home it was as if he had suddenly met up with the man he had known. Victor had decided the verdict was entirely down to Tom's good work, bought him Carling Black Label from the trolley as it passed, and drank it himself when Tom subtly pushed it aside, beaming at him broadly from across the plastic table.

Florence and Belle were nervously pacing about the Penzance platform when they got home, and Tom stood back in wonder, arms folded over his chest, while poor Vic for the first time in years ran to embrace his wife. Later that week Florence scared him by informing him that Vic was now spending more time than ever in his boathouse, but that he was building something—actually working, the sounds of hammering and wood-turning making welcome music in the Porth Bay harbour again.

Tom had to run a double surgery to make up for his one-day closure, every kid in a ten-mile radius apparently having come down with measles overnight, and by the time he crawled back to his refuge on Friday night, he barely had the strength to feed Belle and himself, in that order, and fall into bed.

Where he dreamed of Flynn. His mind had seized on images and would not let them go. Good ones included the kindling light in Flynn's eyes across the breakfast table—ordinary, a thing to be seen every day in a different light, bright enough to Tom to dim the morning sun. Flynn, struggling to his fraught, against-all-odds climax on the sofa. Then there were the bad ones, where, instead of rolling half-drowned and struggling to Tom's feet at Porth Bay, Flynn had come unbreathing, a blue-lipped corpse to his hands. Where Tom was present, a mute ghost in the corner of room six, west barrack, while Flynn acquired his latest set of bruises. Those dreams woke him shuddering.

He got up early on Saturday, restless, aware that a week ago he had been unwittingly on the brink of the strangest, sweetest adventure of his life. Belle had been much neglected over the last few days, and, not allowing himself any concise thoughts on destination or purpose, he bundled her into the Land Rover and set off.

The quoit had sailed a long way adrift of its usual point of anchorage. As usual, Tom tried to persuade himself that it was a trick of the light, which was opalescent this morning, deceiving.

Or perhaps the ancient stones were weary at the thought of the oncoming tourist season. There were only a couple of parking bays off the narrow, ochre-tarmac'd road that led past the quoit, and one of these was already occupied. A sleek little Mazda convertible, about ten years old, shining sea green in the sun. It looked as if it had seen some service, Tom thought, and these roads must be hard on it. Long nose, light chassis. Attractive, but not suitable at all. He registered these things distantly, pulling to a halt in the next bay. At least the quoit and its surrounding moorland were still deserted. Letting Belle half-haul him over the stile in the high-banked wall, rippling with campions and dancing umbellifers, he slipped off her leash and watched her tear away, a grey shadow on the wind.

It was a lonely place. Tom had never felt this before. Shouldering his pack, in which he carried bags to clear up after Belle and, at least as often, human detritus, as well as a small first-aid kit, baby brother to the massive one in the Rover's boot, which he did not seem able to leave behind even on the shortest walk—and water, and sun cream, and, God, how he wished he could sometimes just *go*—he made his way over to the megalith.

He stood in the shadow of its mighty capstone. His ancestors, its builders, would have laughed at him. Would not have recognised, perhaps, this late fruit of their loins as human at all. The wind, which seldom ceased its scouring even on the calmest day up here, sang among the uprights. If he closed his eyes, he saw Flynn's face, tilted up to his and becoming fixed in a kind of wonder as climax swept over him. He felt Flynn's hands, caressing him while they lay in a stunned tangle on the turf. Would he see and feel these things always? His shock at David's death had expunged from him all tactile memory of their one shared night. He had learned to be alone.

Well, not quite. Belle, having finished her flying patrol, was circling back round towards him. He smiled. She wasn't great for conversation, but nor was he, and her affections at least never altered. "Here, Belle, girl," he called, leaning over and patting his knees to intercept her.

She shot past him as if he didn't exist, and headed like an arrow for the stile. Turning in astonishment to watch her, Tom was in time to see Flynn Summers jump lithely down onto the turf.

They approached one another casually. It was all fine. Tom was sure the wild thumping of his heart did not carry over the wind. Flynn was smiling. His long stride ate up the ground unhurriedly. They could have been any two friends meeting up by chance in the May sunshine, and if the catch of the wind in his hair, the power of his movements, was drying Tom's mouth with desire, that symptom could be concealed. Flynn didn't need a rucksack full of kit to go for a walk, did he? Just the clothes he stood up in—dazzling white shirt, jeans if anything more beautifully worn and fitting than the ones he had skinned out of in the watchtower's bedroom a week ago—and his own graceful self. Barely had this yearning thought flashed through Tom's head when Flynn, mindful of anything but his footing, caught his ankle in a clump of tough long grass and fell over, flinging out both hands to stop himself from measuring his length on the turf.

Tom's concern—and sobriety—lasted as long at it took Flynn to stand up, brushing at the grass stains on his knees. He looked up at Tom, who had pressed a hand to his mouth in a poor attempt to conceal laughter. He shook his head, called out, "That's like falling off the platform edge in *Brief Encounter*," and resumed his course.

Belle wove a couple of joyful figures of eight around them, then somehow the last few yards disappeared all at once. Tom had one flash of *Brief Encounter's* Laura pelting out of the station café after a vanishing train, and then he was clasped in Flynn's arms, clinging to his shirt, one hand starfishing over his hair, as if they'd been torn apart at birth.

Inexplicable. Tom heard his own ragged breathing, which threatened to crack into sobs, and tried to find perspective, sense. He'd known him for a fortnight, not his whole bloody life. They'd had one night. And he was… "Flynn," he gasped, struggling reluctantly out of the kiss which was bearing him back against the quoit's huge southern upright. "I'm not scared of bloody Robert Tremaine…"

Flynn snorted faintly. "I'll say. He was white to his gills. What did you do?"

"…but I'm not about to mess with him, or you, if you're still involved."

They had subsided onto the turf in the megalith's shadow. Flynn's gaze on him was luminous, his grasp deep and hungry. His eyelashes were caught together with tears, which might have been stung there by the wind, but his voice too was unsteady as he said, "God, Tom. You're so warm. You're—real, real as the earth. I've never wanted anything as much as I want you now."

Tom swallowed. But he was deadly serious. He knew that Rob Tremaine's backlash, whatever form it took, would hit Flynn first, if they were still tied. "Flynn. I mean it."

"I know. I finished it. It's over."

Tom let go. He hauled a breath of the intoxicating air and let the sunlight evaporate the last traces of his fear. If he was hearing what he wanted to hear, so be it—for once in his life he would allow himself the luxury, and believe it too. He reached up, smiling, and gave himself over into Flynn's hands.

"I thought… You told me not to trust any man, to let him do this unprotected."

Tom shivered. Flynn's whisper was hot against his ear. His trousers were down round his thighs, at whose instigation he couldn't quite recall, and Flynn was behind him, ready. He heard his own words, echoing round his stone bedchamber. They were just as true out here in the sun but he somehow couldn't feel them. All he could feel was the warmth and the push of Flynn's body as he angled him, took hold of his hips in his hands. He was on his knees, chest and belly lightly pressed against the quoit's upright, hands grasping at its grey flanks, which were warm as a beast's in the sun. His ice was melting—the outer layer, which calmed his fears by distraction, pouring all his energies into countless domestic repetitive tasks, and the deep inner core, which defended him from all loss of control. Which kept him safe and frozen away from such events as unprotected sex with a relative stranger at the foot of a public monument.

He said faintly, "I know. But I do trust you. There's… There's some sun cream in my pack."

He laid his brow to the stone and closed his eyes as Flynn pushed into him. The cream wasn't the best lubricant, even liberally applied, even rubbed inside his body on the tips of clever fingers whose probing, stroking touch he had had to beg to be reprieved from before he made a fool of himself. It hurt. The stretch, and then the inner straining hurt him badly for a second, and he jolted and his hands made involuntary fists on the stone. But it was simply that he had been lonely and unused, and Flynn, after an attentive pause, kissing his neck, gently squeezing his upright cock, had gone on.

In the red-flashing dark behind his eyelids, Tom remembered how he had looked, how he had risen up like sunrise on his sofa, and envisaged that long, powerful shaft disappearing into him, higher and higher, inch by inch. He spread his thighs. He was almost straddling the stone, his cock lightly brushing it as Flynn pushed. When he came, he would come on it. He shuddered, felt himself almost break apart in choked laughter and bitten-back moans. Would the old gods tip the capstone down on top of them in wrath, or would they rejoice with him? Too far gone to mind, Tom got his head up for one look across the moor. Still deserted, and Belle was keeping watch, but that wouldn't have mattered either.

Flynn found full reach inside him and began to ride him hard. Tom knew that he had within himself a compact, sturdy strength, diminished a little by the way he had been living but still there to call upon. His barricades down, he could brace, open himself up and let Flynn in, so receptive now he thought the delicious inward press would go on forever. His white-knuckle clench on the rock unfolded as he relaxed. Flynn placed one hand on top of his, and Tom heard him gasp as he seized it, interweaving their fingers, straining back, twisting round to seek a kiss.

"God, Tom! Don't!"

"What?"

"Rob never… Oh, Christ, the most I get from him when we do this is a slap to the hip, like I was a well-trained horse or…"

"Forget him," Tom growled. Flynn kissed him, briefly, fiercely, and he grabbed his free hand and pulled it round to clasp his cock. He could feel inside him the rhythmic pulse of muscle that signalled the finish, and he loosed a deep, raw shout, throwing his head back onto Flynn's shoulder. He wanted to draw it out—feel, for as long as either of them could stand it, Flynn's long strokes in and out of his core, making him buck his spine and rump powerfully back to meet him—but it was all he could do to hold on till Flynn hit his brink, groaning through gritted teeth.

His last launching thrust drove Tom against the rock, grazing his belly and chest. Flynn rasped out his name, shuddering seismically against his back, pinning him—felt his muscle ring contract tight then begin a hot flutter round the base of Flynn's shaft. For an instant Tom was afraid—of the force of what was happening, to him and to this perfect, fever-driven lover, whose desperate spending he could feel in him like rushing spring meltwater—that it would break both their backs or their hearts to get through this—but Flynn's hand tightened hard on him, and he burst to a pleasure so bright that it put out the sun.

***

Mustn't go to sleep here. Tom's week had been long, and the rich May sunlight, in this sheltered corner of the world, was almost irresistible. He tried to lift his head from Flynn's shoulder, but his companion's drowsy murmur drew him back. "Tom…"

"Yes." He turned and pressed an exhausted kiss to Flynn's neck. "Still here, I think. Are you okay?"

"Yes, I think. I don't know."

Tom shifted a little, far enough to look at him. There had been pain as well as joy in his climaxing shout. "What is it, love?"

Flynn twitched. "Oh, don't. Don't call me…"

Tom, from whom the endearment had fallen truly but easily, stroked his chest. "All right."

"I mean, I want you to, but—I'm not entirely loveable."

"Matter of perspective," Tom told him, smiling. "And opinion. What's eating you? Does it bear talking about?"

"If you don't mind listening to a big sap."

"It's what I live for. Come on."

"Okay. You asked for it." Tom bit back the moan of contentment that would have distracted him, as Flynn tightened both arms around him and eased his tired, reverberating flesh against his own. "Rob and I do that—I mean, we have done, obviously, and it wasn't like that. I didn't know it could be."

Tom listened. He caught his lip between his teeth and pretended to be giving it thought. His heart was bumping with surprise and pleasure. "Mm, yes," he said after a moment. "That is a very, very big sap."

"Screw you," Flynn growled at him, laughter flickering in the muscles under Tom's hand. "Last time I confide in you."

"Flynn?"

"What, love?"

"Do they *make* you live in bunk two, room six? Is it like a…"

"A condition of my parole? No. It was just where I landed. Why?"

"Come and land with me for a while. For… For as long as you like."

A silence fell. During it, Tom wondered if he had gone too far. Already he was astonished at what he had offered, or what he had dared say aloud, but he could see it, clearly as he could remember the night on which he had opened up at last the impregnable tower in which he lived. Bringing Flynn back through that door, securing it behind them. Seeing last summer light in the round chamber, following Flynn up to bed. Waking beside him that morning, and who knew how many mornings after. As many as he could possibly squeeze out of his time on earth. He swallowed hard as the prospect of death, which had danced like luring swamp lights round the edges of his mind since Afghanistan, became suddenly what it had been to him before—a necessity, not to be feared, but staved off as long as possible in the interests of life.

Flynn drew a breath, and somehow Tom heard in it all his uncertainty. He sat up, knelt in front of him. "Don't," he said softly. "Don't say anything. It's there if you want it, that's all."

"I do. I do, but I have to… Rob's away on leave this week, and I can't just ditch out on him. Let me just—"

"No. No promises." Tom stood up stiffly, feeling the tug of long-unused muscles, and put out a hand for him. "Come on. Walk my dog with me. I'll buy you lunch somewhere." Flynn struggled upright, and stood staring at him as if dazed. "It's not a thing to hurt you, Flynn. It's just there if you want."

Chapter Seven
Vortex

Tom lay on his side in the round upper room, looking at the vacant half of the bed beside him. He was awake but not restless. The sea music that always resonated here was quiet tonight.

If he put out a hand, he could almost imagine a trace of body warmth in the sheets. He had thought Flynn was going to come back with him, after their walk and lunch up at the Mermaid in Zennor. The little green Mazda had turned out to be his, so low in Tom's rearview she sometimes disappeared as he led the way along the snaking cliff-top road. They had sat outside, the tables round them too crowded now for anything other than general conversation, but even that had felt good. A taste of ordinary life. Flynn's foot had rested lightly against his.

There had been a moment in the sunny car park afterward, when many things had seemed to hang in the balance. Then Flynn's eyes had darkened with an anxiety Tom would not have added to for the world, and he had risked both their reputations, pulling Flynn into the shelter of the Land Rover to kiss him. "It's all right," Tom had told him again, the reassurance formless but broad, and he had watched with a weird, painful clutch at his heart while Flynn drove away.

He allowed himself to imagine how it might have been, otherwise. Flynn was not hard to conjure. Tom could feel the shape of him inside, a vivid memory. Even the slight soreness was a source of pleasure. Alone, he blushed and felt a smile crease his mouth at the sensation of having been richly and memorably ploughed… They would have come back here, and straight upstairs this time. If Flynn was healed, he would have tumbled him straight down onto the bedspread and… And that brought Tom too close to thoughts of pain, injury, Robert bloody Tremaine, who, away on leave or not, could make Flynn twitch with nerves whenever anyone of similar build and colouring had come near their table at the Mermaid, so he reversed it, let the fantasy meet the physical echo, the velvety stretch inside him.

Unexpectedly, some inner wall fell. Before Flynn, it was David who had fucked him last. Lieutenant David Reay, assistant army medical officer, on the 28th of January three years gone, in a bunk room in Camp Bastion. These details, which rushed over Tom in an unstoppable dam-burst of memory, should have paralysed him. Balled him up hopelessly in the bed, snatching at the duvet to drag over his head and obliterate him, and then, when they became unbearable, send him stumbling downstairs to tear open a bottle. He had got round all this recently by ceasing to think of David at all, and he had called this avoidance a form of adaptation, healing.

Not Flynn on top of him, opening him with gentle, unsteady fingers, pushing inside. David. David had been so pent-up it hadn't lasted long. Tom had felt the frantic thrusting and rush of his coming before he was even properly engaged, and then the poor sod had been so mortified, sitting hunched on the edge of the bunk with his head in his hands. Tom had teased him, gently, and persuaded him back for another go, and things had been better after that. For one night, most of which Tom had spent with one eye fixed on the bunk-room door. David had waited for him for three years, and Tom had not given him so much as his full attention.

Falling walls. Pain swept through Tom, and he turned his inner vision back to Flynn, whose arrival in his life, whose touch and voice, had brought them down and yet somehow made the consequences bearable. Because Tom was holding on. He was remembering. Flynn became David, then himself again, and merged, and Tom placed a chilled, sweat-damped hand on his own cock and caressed himself to hardness and sudden orgasm, tearing and sweet, way too soon. He could taste blood from his own bitten lip, blood and salt from his tears. Sleep instantly seized him. He heard a voice—David's, Flynn's, he did not know. It said—that old lie, but Tom was floating painlessly in the truth of it—*it's all right, love.*

***

The phone rang two hours later, jolting him out of his sleep's deepest cycle. Moaning, he got his head up out of the pillows and shoved onto one elbow, mouth dry, heart thumping. Penzance Casualty on the caller ID. He grabbed for the receiver. "God almighty. *What?*"

"Tom, it's Mike. I'm sorry. We've had some kind of boat wreck—gunshot wounds, near-drownings. Looks like a couple of drug-running gangs had a set-to. And a pileup on the A30. Can you possibly…?"

Tom was already out of bed, reaching for the shirt he'd left crumpled on the floor in Flynn's honour. His supper dishes were unwashed downstairs, as well. It had been a day of freedom. "I'll be there," he said, and hung up. *Peaceful bloody Cornwall*, he thought, distractedly, grabbing jeans and car keys, running for the stairs.

***

An ex-army doctor was a blessing to an overstretched rural casualty department, and Tom was sure of a fervent welcome on nights like this. The casualty consultant, Mike Findlay, grabbed him by the arm as soon as he appeared in the chaotic assessment unit and pointed him straight at the car-crash victims. Nature and experience had combined in Tom to make him a kindly, absolutely dispassionate force for good, and he dealt with broken children, blood and horror much better than some of Mike's full-time casualty staff. Tonight, if Mike had been looking, he might have seen an unprecedented tremor in his swiftly working hands, might have noticed that, for once, he was pale—but there was no time for observation, for anything other than the frantic dash from trolley to incoming trolley.

The pile-up had happened just after the arrival of six bits of human wreckage from some kind of boat collision off Morvanna point. Two separate small craft had been involved, the violence of the impact suggesting to observers—a handful of shocked night fishermen on the pier—that it had been deliberate. Shots had been fired. Officers from the armed-response unit in Exeter were waiting in the hospital corridors until they could question the survivors.

No one had deliberately prioritised the pileup over what was probably fallout from a trafficking war. Neither Findlay nor Tom would have allowed it, any more than Tom had ever succumbed to pressure from his army superiors to deal with non-urgent Allied troops before critically injured Afghanis. It was simply that the crash victims were greater in number and more inclined to die, and by the time the casualty staff had stemmed some of this tide, the men from the boat collision had been set up in a side ward, under the care of stressed nurses and anyone else who could be called in from their off duty. When the worst of the crisis in the main wards had passed, Tom went through to see what he could do to help.

He found that he was looking around for Flynn. This was the kind of nightmare that would call out the rescue choppers, and the Maritime Security Lynxes too. Unease pulled at him. He had not considered, when opening his fortress, how it would be to have someone in there with him whom he could not protect, someone as vulnerable in his own way as David had been.

"Did the Hawke Lake SAR bring this lot in?" he asked one of the nurses, but the woman shook her head. It had happened so close to shore that the lifeboat and a police launch had gone out to pick up the bits. They'd found assault rifles on board, and a small fortune in cocaine. "Great," Tom said wryly. "Bet they don't put that in the Penwith visitors' guide. Do they need help mopping up?"

"You could relieve Dr. Francis. She's been on for eighteen hours."

The man in the first side-ward bed had third-degree burns and a bullet wound to his arm. Either he spoke no English or had found it expedient to forget what he knew. Tom could see the coppers out in the corridor, restlessly pacing up and down. Well, they could wait. Until the man's fever came down, he was a patient, not a prisoner, no matter what his sins. He did what he could for him and moved on to the next bed.

No one had got round to cleaning this one up. He wasn't high priority, his injuries not severe, just bashed across the head with a rifle butt in the fight, brought in to sleep it off and be arrested in due course. He looked as if he'd been in oil-slicked water, his hair matted, black stains obscuring his features. He was lying on his side in the ward's farthest corner. When Tom touched his shoulder, he came round immediately. His eyes flicked wide and fixed themselves on the wall.

To Tom's surprise, his first emotion was not astonishment or disgust. Christ, that would do it, wouldn't it? A couple of wrong-side runs like this, with his insider knowledge, would buy plenty of Mercedes trucks, and free exit forever from the Sankerris Bay estate. No, it was pity that went through Tom, a wave of compassion—as well as shame, because had he not too, from boyhood, contributed to the social pressures that would lead a man like this to... "Tremaine," he whispered. "Are you mixed up in this? For God's sake, let me help you."

The grey eyes remained wide and vacant, the profile impassive. Tom drew breath to try again—but the shrill of a flat-lining heart monitor cut through the air from the main ward, the one sound that could have distracted him, and he ran to answer Mike Findlay's shout.

When he got back, the bed was empty. Only rumpled sheets and oil stains. Tom shook his head. Had he been dreaming? On reflection, it seemed unlikely, didn't it, Rob Tremaine brought in with a bunch of gun-runners. Still, whatever the situation, he'd lost a patient—his first tonight, somehow. Half-smiling at the idea of losing one like this, Tom checked the toilets at the end of the ward, then went into the corridor where the weary-looking police officers were still waiting. "You brought in six, didn't you?" he asked.

The Kevlar-clad armed-response captain stopped trying to extract a packet of crisps from the vending machine. "Yeah," he said. "Why?"

"I'm down to five. Anyone come past you this way?"

"No. Which one's gone?"

"The head injury. He's..." Abruptly Tom shut up. He saw again the raw-boned profile, half covered with hair and black grease. God, was he absolutely sure? If not, it was a hell of an accusation to make. It flickered through Tom's mind that Tremaine might have been undercover, although he did not think Hawke would send one of its pilots on a job like this.

"He's what?"

"He's too sick to be running around. I'll call security."

"Yeah," said the officer, grimly, unhitching his radio. "Me too.

***

I promised him I wouldn't turn up outside his barrack door. Tom sat behind the wheel of the Land Rover. His parking place commanded a view up and down the Breagh main street. It was just after three in the afternoon, the time when Flynn would come off a duty shift if he'd been on early. Tom knew he liked to get off the base for a couple of hours a day, and if he did, he had to drive through the village. If not, he thought, gripping the wheel painfully tight, it might come to a barrack-door encounter yet.

Tom was not sure he would have bothered, had it just been drugs and guns. *Just*, he had said to himself mockingly, trying to get some sleep in that day's bright dawn, back at the watchtower. But the truth was that he was not much concerned with issues of crime and punishment for their own sake. He was a doctor. His job began where those of the police and firearms units ended. Ultimately it wasn't his business if Rob Tremaine or anyone else chose to make a few illicit quid by running with the moonrakers. And, as he had realised when talking to the police last night, he hadn't been absolutely certain, not certain enough to shadow an innocent man's career.

He supposed he was slow on the uptake. At the best interpretation, he was these days an unsuspicious man, too occupied with getting through his own day-to-day to be curious about anyone else's. It had taken hours for the fear to hit him. He had been opening up the surgery, had gone so cold that he had dropped the keys and almost set the pharmacy alarm off. Had conducted his appointments in a grey distraction, glad that nothing more complex than a grumbling appendix presented itself. He had listened, diagnosed, dispensed, sent the appendix down to Penzance for assessment, closed shop as soon as he could and driven over to Breagh.

What the hell was he going to say?

A throaty purring preceded the appearance of Flynn's sea-green Mazda at the top of the high street. For a moment, Tom forgot everything. Flynn looked like a bloody advert—the convertible's top was down, the sunny breeze catching his hair, glancing off his aviator sunglasses. Tom rolled down the Rover's window and put out a hand to attract his attention, but there was no need—Flynn had seen him from a hundred yards away, the light show of his recognition once more dazzling to Tom, who could not get used to being greeted with such unhidden pleasure.

Anxiety under it today. For all their short acquaintance, Tom had begun to be able to read him, even at a distance. It matched the dry clutch of fear in his own throat. Flynn pulled the Mazda into the car park outside the Fox, gesturing for Tom to follow him. Well, no help for it. Either Tom spoke to him about this now or not at all, and *not at all* was suddenly unbearable to him.

***

They found a table in a quiet corner. The Fox was a different place during weekday work hours, Tom observed with relief, hearing the echo of roaring voices and feeling a sting in his healed-over knuckles. Flynn had met him with the reserved affection which was all he would ever be able to show in public, military man to village doctor, in such a community, and Tom found himself wishing them both a thousand miles away, stripped of rank, status, for preference every stitch of clothing, and alone. His heart was racing, his hands unsteady on the glass of orange juice Flynn had brought back from the bar. "Hiya," Tom greeted him, as calmly as he could. "You all right?"

Flynn sat down opposite him. When he looked up, there was such a mix of yearning and fear in his eyes that Tom almost blew it all by reaching for his hands across the table, under the attentive gaze of the bartender and the dozen or so RNAS regulars scattered around the room. "I'm fine," he said. "Hear you were busy last night, though."

"Yes. Couple of boats rammed each other off Morvanna." He smiled, desperately trying to keep it light. "Bodies all over the place. Police think… Police think it was a couple of rival drug warlords knocking heads." Tom clenched his hands together on the table. He stared at his own white knuckles for almost ten seconds, then asked hoarsely, "Flynn, love. Is Robert all right?"

"I… What? Yeah, he's fine. Why would he not be? That is… I dunno. He's on leave."

You're a rotten liar, aren't you? Tom thought, with a painful surge of affection. He had worked that much out back at the quoit, where Flynn had only got away with his declaration of freedom from Rob Tremaine because they had both so badly wanted it to be true. To have to probe at him, to question, was terrible. "You've heard from him?"

"Yes. I mean… Oh Christ." Flynn picked up his glass—he too was on the orange juice, a tactful gesture which, given his current levels of anxiety, Tom appreciated all the more—sent the top inch of its contents over the brim, and set it back down again. Tom shoved a napkin at him, and together they tried to mop up without attracting too much notice. "All right. He came home early this morning. I wasn't expecting him. Why?"

"And he was okay?"

"No. He was tired. He looked…" Flynn ran a hand into his hair. "He looked the way you do now. Leave it to me, Tom. I'll fuck everyone over, every time."

"Does he ever work undercover? Could you tell me if he did?"

"What? No. I mean—I probably couldn't, but he doesn't. Please tell me why you're asking."

"Because…" *Because if it was just a fling from time to time, a run with the wolves, I might look away. Whatever that makes me. A sideline like that would keep a man in Mercedes trucks, for sure. But private psychiatry, legal fees—the price of a human soul, lock, stock and barrel—that takes more.* "Because I need you to tell me what happened the night your helicopter went down off Portsmouth."

"I did tell you." Flynn's voice was strained, barely audible. Tears had sprung to his eyes. "I told you all I remember. Don't do this. Please."

"I'd give anything not to have to. Flynn. How did Robert get out of that crash? How could he have?"

Flynn's chair scraped. Heads turned. Tom, opening up his hands to stare into their palms, did not watch his exit, which was quick and silent. He sat for as long as he could bear to, his drink untouched on the table. Then he got up, put his jacket over his arm, and just as quietly left the bar.

How stupid. His vision was blurring, his chest tight. Pit of his stomach clenching, with grief and a kind of sick rage—if he had to lose this, lose Flynn, why had it had to be by his own hand? Realising that for the first time in his adult life he was on the verge of public tears, he backed up into a shadowy part of the corridor outside the bar. He tried a few deep breaths. Not once, not in all his battles, had he ever been brought this low. *Shit*, he thought, hot wet salt burning up his throat, and he made his way blindly across the corridor to the toilets.

Empty, thank God. Shuddering, Tom jerked one of the basin's cold taps onto full and leaned over, splashing handfuls of water into his face. When he straightened up, he could see again. The fittings in the room were basic, unchanged, he reckoned, since the pub first opened in the late seventies to cater to the airbase. In the single mirror screwed to the wall, his image stared back at him, an insignificant ghost—one of thousands that had stood here, drunk or sober, in the thick of life or beached and lost, or simply bored. All meaningless. Tom could hardly assign enough importance to the reflection to wonder at it. Pale skin, dark eyes. Wet fringe plastered down. The whole face a blank, the water on it now nothing worse than clean Cornish tap. Unreadable. He would be all right now, or at least he would be able to get back to the car.

The door creaked. Tom turned from the mirror, ready to make his exit past a stranger, and found himself face-to-face with Flynn. "Oh," he said, his own voice sounding odd to him, flat and detached. "I'm glad you came back. I—"

"You shouldn't be," Flynn interrupted. He was a little out of breath, as if he had come running back from his car. He looked sick, almost ready to pass out. "You shouldn't be glad to see me. Christ, Tom." He closed the door behind him, gave the room a cursory glance to check that they were alone, and came up close. He scanned Tom's face. "I made you cry."

"No," Tom whispered. He couldn't bear for him to think so. He wanted to resist Flynn's hands on him—the unsteady caress down the side of his face, the touch to his arm—because whatever

Flynn had come back to tell him, it wasn't that he was there to stay. "Ah, Flynn. What is it? Please tell me."

"I will. That's why I'm here. I fucked you around. I lied to you about me and Rob. We're not over."

"I know."

"You… When? From the start?" Flynn asked. Tom nodded mutely, and Flynn closed his eyes for a second, losing even more colour. "Why did you let me…do what we did?"

"Same reason you did. I wanted you more than anything. I still do."

"No. That's just it. You don't know me, Tom. You're right— Rob came back in a fucking state last night. Like a hurricane. He'd been in a fight, and…" He ground to a halt, stripping off his jacket. Tom shuddered and tried to step back, but the marks on Flynn leapt out like a cry—fingerprint bruises up and down his arms, fresh, terrible, purple and dark blue against his tan. "I won't show you the rest. He came back, and he took it all out on me, just like he stamped his bloody mark on me for a week when you first showed up, like he could read my bloody mind. He did it because he likes it, and because…" Flynn paused, sucked in a breath. "Because I need him to. You don't understand, Tom. You're too good, too clean, too *decent*, to get your head around the kind of sick fuck I am. He beats the crap out of me, screws me until I can't walk, and sometimes—just *sometimes*, just for a little bit—I feel better about what I am. What… What I did."

"Oh, Flynn. Flynn, for God's sake, listen to me." Tom heard his voice crack. Flynn's eyes were fixed on his, their gaze burning and blank and desperate. "You're not sick. You're just hurt. And I—I'm starting to think none of what happened that night was your fault."

"No. Shut up. Whatever you think about Rob, it's not true. He roughs me up, but he'd never harm anyone else. Christ, he'd never *kill* anyone."

"All right. Okay, but just tell me… He'd been in a fight?"

"Yes. He told me all about it. He had some kind of a bust-up with his family, so he came back early, and he got pissed down in Penzance and picked a scrap with a bunch of Royal Marines. Happens all the time—they think SAR is for pansies. He…"

"Flynn." Tom grabbed him by the arms. He had no interest whatsoever in the Navy's internecine rivalries, and less in Rob Tremaine's lies. He saw, with nausea, that his own thumbs fitted exactly into the place where Rob had left bruises, and he transferred his grip to Flynn's shoulders, caressing. "Right. Listen. Did he have a head wound? Quite bad, at the back of his skull?"

"Oh Christ!" Flynn tore away from him. He fell back a couple of steps, throwing out a hand to steady himself on the edge of a washbasin. "How the fuck should I know? It was dark, and he bust in before I was even awake. He had his cock up my arse before I could get my face out of the pillow. He…" Running out of breath, Flynn emitted a faint sound of pain and disgust, as if the reality of the scene he was describing had only then hit home. He swallowed audibly, a sickened small moan. "Oh. Tom…"

"It's all right. It'll be all right, if you just let me help you. Where is he now?"

"He's on duty. Where else would he be? Tom, I can't do this. And—I don't know what *you're* trying to do. Rob fucks me over, but I need him." He went a shade paler and swung round to face the sink. "Has that occurred to you? I *need* him, even—even more than I need you."

Tom took a step towards him. Pain was lancing through him. He put a hand on Flynn's shoulder, feeling it shudder with a hard-repressed dry heave. "Flynn. All right. Forget it. Just…how badly are you hurt? I can ignore everything else, but not that. I—I'm a doctor."

"I've got my own doctor!" It was a desperate snarl. Flynn straightened up violently, pushing him aside. "I'm not your responsibility. Not your business. Nor is Rob. For both our sakes…" he backed up unsteadily, and did not look at Tom again until he was at the door, "…leave me alone. It's over. Let me go."

***

Tom left the pub calmly, dry-eyed. He got into the Rover and started her up with steady hands. Down the street, he could hear the roar of the little MX5, getting booted to high speeds as Flynn took her out of the 30 zone. Tom wanted to call him back, to tell him to be careful.

He was careful himself, driving home. He had good reason. He was going to have to choose, very soon, between two distinct courses of action. He could walk into the Penzance police HQ, find the officer in charge of the boat-crash investigation and tell him that, on slender evidence, he thought their missing sixth man was Robert Tremaine—that, further, he believed Tremaine capable of deliberately downing an RNAS helicopter, capable of doing it again. If it had been Tremaine in the side ward last night, he would have a distinctive head injury. Tom could do this. He could probably throw enough suspicion on Tremaine to ground him at least.

Ruin his career, and shatter Flynn, perhaps beyond healing. Tom's other choice was to shut the fuck up and watch from a distance. If Tremaine hadn't sabotaged the Portsmouth helicopter, he had seen its destruction, and Flynn's, at close quarters. He was the only witness. He had seen to the repairs, put Flynn back together as nearly as he could in his own image. Right or wrong,

Tom knew that, to all intents and purposes, Tremaine owned him. Loss of that ownership, that domination, might set Flynn free. Or cut through his strings like a scythe.

Whichever Tom chose, it would wait until morning. It would have to. Beneath all this concern for the greater human good, his own grief and loss were yawning like a pit.

When the hell had he fallen in love?

***

Another vehicle was parked on the turf outside the watchtower. Tom watched it with a sinking sense of disbelief. Apart from Flynn—and, of course, Tremaine—he had received no social calls since moving in. It was not a place where people dropped by. He didn't even recognise the rusty Ford hatchback. Didn't much care. Whoever it was, to Tom, they were simply an obstacle between him and the pit, where he did not want to fall but was losing the strength to hold on.

He got out of the Rover, and Victor Travers unfolded his bulk from behind the wheel of the other car, waving. "Tom," he called. "Sorry to disturb you out here. I know you don't like visitors."

God, when had he given that impression? It was true enough—or had been—but how had he made his aversion so plain? A notice tin-tacked to the tree on Sankerris village green? He made his way over to Victor, out of habit running through the visual checks he would have begun had his old friend just entered the surgery. No tremor, no weight loss. In fact, he looked as if he'd glued a little on, his huge frame less gaunt in its flesh. His colour was good. Tom realised he did know the Ford estate, after all. Vic's dad had driven it around Porth Harbour for years, usually with ladders and pots of creosote hanging out the back. It was just that he hadn't seen it in three years. Because Vic, having had the living crap land-mined out of him twice behind the wheel of an armoured truck, had not been able to drive.

Despite himself, Tom smiled. "Hi, Vic. You okay? Prescription run out?"

A shadow touched Victor's grin. "Don't blame you for thinking that. Been a right millstone round your neck since we got home, haven't I? No, I... The missus sent me out to see you were okay, actually. She said you looked like grim death this morning in surgery."

"In surgery? I don't think I saw her."

"Maybe not. But you did a nice job of fixing her ingrown toenail anyway."

Tom shook his head. Yes. He remembered a human foot, some swelling, inflammation, the few strokes it took with a pair of nail shears to put it right. They didn't have their own chiropodist in Sankerris—he got the odd job like that. A human foot attached to a leg, attached to a familiar woman in a bright floral dress, looking at him in concern. "Sorry. Yes, I did see her. I was miles away."

"Is something the matter, Tom? Florrie says you got into a punch-up with one of the lads from the airbase the other week."

God, not you too. "Florrie says too much," he said grimly, and then regretted it. "Sorry, Vic. Bad day. You want to come in and talk?"

Vic looked down at Tom from the foot of height he had on him. His expression was thoughtful. "No. I think I've pretty much talked you to death over the last few years, haven't I? And I know you have bad days." He reached out, put a large hand on Tom's shoulder and awkwardly squeezed it. "Just wanted to see you were all right. Come down and have dinner with me and Florrie some night, okay?"

Tom watched him depart. It struck him that both he and Victor had been chasing mirages out there in the Middle East. Vic had wanted excitement, adventure, and he himself…

Opening the door to the tower, distractedly greeting Belle, Tom tried to remember what he had joined up for. Just to bring the benefit of his medical skills to the front line? Hardly, although he had wanted to change things, make something out there better. He had been lonely—looking for just the kind of comradeship which had two minutes ago presented itself to him outside his own front door. Which had doubtless been here all the time, if he'd been brave enough to look. But he hadn't been brave. He'd been shy, too chained up even to accept the bright and unreserved love David Reay had laid in his lap.

Shy, stupid, blind. Sure of his own sexuality, too scared to take it with him into the army. Even if he was inclined to damn poor Flynn for cowardice, who was he to talk? He didn't have a leg to stand on.

And now Vic was gone, Belle fed and given her hour's runaround on the cliff tops. Tom looked around his home, which, for once during his occupation of it, could really use a cleanup. The undone dishes, the sheets he hadn't been able to bring himself to change since Flynn's brief visitation to his solitary bed, the books and newspapers scattered round the living room—all these had been his friends before, or handholds at least, when he was trying to stay out of the pit.

Locking the back and front doors behind him, securing his prison, Tom admitted to himself that he wasn't trying at all. He sat on the sofa, and after a minute picked up the receiver of the phone. He was aware that he was struggling not to ball up, to wrap his arms around himself, and stopped it. It was cold in here, that was all. He dialled the number of the locum doctor he shared with the surgeries in Newlyn and St. Just. Yes, she was available to cover for him tomorrow. That was good, Tom told her, absently pushing Belle away as she poked an anxious, food-speckled nose beneath his arm. He'd been called away unexpectedly—it would only be the one day.

And surely Flynn should be safe for that amount of time, shouldn't he? Until Tom emerged? He and Tremaine didn't fly together anymore, were in different branches of the service. No, he should be fine. Locked into a barrack room, beaten up and fucked raw, which was what he appeared to want. Fine…

The Stoli Elit was better chilled. Tom reckoned, if he gave it half an hour, he could almost disguise this oncoming bender from himself as a few pleasant drinks. The first part of it, anyway. And he was not so desperate, was he, that he couldn't put the bottle in the fridge and wait for thirty bloody minutes? He stood in the kitchen, rolling the bottle, with its bright contents and shining silver label, between his palms.

Rage shook him. No, he couldn't bloody wait. He was an addict, same as any bored housewife he tried to wean off sedatives or any junkie kid on the Penzance estates. An addict, a drunk, without even that last shred of self-control he could use to hide from his own shame. Without warning, the muscles in his arms and shoulders tensed—the same involuntary spasm that had pitched Rob Tremaine off his back and onto the cobbles at the Fox—and he found himself smashing the bottle down on the edge of the sink.

It did not so much break as explode. Tom stood at the end of his action, staring dully at the floor. He tried to be so gentle, didn't he? A doctor. But he didn't know his own strength. Given opportunity, motive, he could be just as much of a ham-fisted brute as Tremaine. If the bastard were here now, he would show him. Pull him off Flynn. Slam him down among the shards and batter him to death and beyond, rather than ever let him lay a hand on Flynn again.

The old flagstones were glimmering like a night sky. Hypnotic. A good idea. The raw ethanol evaporating off the spilled vodka rose into his brain. Shivering, Tom dragged a hand across his eyes and stumbled back into the darkness where the tower's stairs coiled down.

The second and third bottles came easy to his hands. He smashed them one after the other on the edge of the sink, this time feeling a kind of scarlet relief as the flying shards bounced back to slice at his palms and wrists. Blood joined the constellations and the vertiginous mess on the floor. He'd kicked his muddy boots off when he came in—did not notice, going back for a fourth, that he was barefoot, that the glass pierced his soles.

A terrible sound brought him to a halt. It was like a child's wail, except that no human throat could have made it. Tom wheeled round, grabbing at the table to stop himself from falling. For a moment there was nothing but his own fractured breathing and the drip of vodka on the flags—and then he saw his dog huddled against the kitchen's far wall. Trying to press herself through the stonework. Eyes wild, hackles raised… She was keening at him in absolute terror.

Tom let go a breath. "Oh, God. Belle." He put the fourth bottle down on the table carefully. There was a bloodstained handprint on it, another on the scratched deal table's surface. Choking faintly, Tom glanced at his hands, made a distracted effort to wipe them on the backside of his jeans. "Belle, sweetheart." He took a step towards her, and she cringed from him.

He didn't know her background, what had happened to her before she had been rescued. The shelter had her history, but Tom hadn't wanted to know, unable at that time to bear the knowledge of further cruelty or pain. Whatever it had been, he knew that he could be kind enough with her, patient and peaceful enough, to make it better. He crouched beside her. He was aware, from a great distance, that he was sobbing, great rough gasps that tore his chest.

"Oh, *Belle*." When finally she let him touch her, he collapsed against the wall at her side. He drew his knees up, folded his arms across the top of his head. He could not breathe or see. The smell of blood and vodka filled his lungs; the sounds of his own grief flooded his ears. Balled up, clutching blindly at the dog's scruff with one hand, he wept, unable to believe the depth, the age, of the wounds gaping wide in him. What was he becoming? What had he already let himself become? The red tide swept through him, through and through, convulsing him until he began to retch dryly and see stars, and even then there was no stopping it, not for a long time, not until he wore himself out and exhaustion at last came to his rescue. His last awareness was of feeling his limbs go slack, of sliding wearily down onto the ancient chilly bones of the watchtower and closing his eyes.

***

The cool rush of wind-driven rain on glass brought him round. He opened his eyes and stared for a long time at the kitchen window, where silver-grey streaks were appearing, sudden bright patterns that destroyed themselves and flickered back, an endless repeat that soothed him.

It occurred to him that he was seeing the pane from an odd angle. A slight kilt off landscape, like a badly hung picture. He normally watched it in dignified perpendicular from his breakfast table. When he tried to correct the orientation, he became aware that his neck was hurting. That there was a sting in his hands and arms like the results of his long-ago tussle with a jellyfish off Porth Bay beach. That he was in fact curled up on his kitchen floor, and that things would have been a lot worse had Belle not forgiven him and lain down with her warm bulk between his spine and the wall.

He sat up with a grunt. The hot spell had broken, a silvery rainstorm now dancing round the tower. The shifting light gleamed dully on a thousand bits of broken glass smashed over the kitchen's flagstones. He croaked, "Jesus Christ," shoving himself upright. He put out a hand to the dog. "Belle. Paw."

She wasn't hurt, somehow. He checked each one of her feet, spreading the hairy pads. Ordering her to stay, he scrambled up, finding out as he did so that he didn't share Belle's discretion or her tough soles. He'd cut himself to ribbons, left a carnage of foot and handprints everywhere. He made the safest track he could to the little utility room, pulled a broom from it and began a swift, dry-mouthed clear-up, brushing the glass into shimmering heaps. The pain in his feet was extraordinary. He took a clinical interest in it, moving back and forth, back and forth, until every shard was swept up, bagged, wrapped in newspaper so the collection men wouldn't do themselves an injury, and dumped in the outside bin. Then he took the vacuum cleaner round. Powdered glass was worse than fragments; got into dog food and water, swallowed, inhaled...

This much accomplished, he sank onto one of the kitchen chairs. He stretched out a hand in a gesture which meant Belle could move, and felt a surge of guilty relief when she came to him without hesitation. In her canine mind, then, everything forgiven and forgotten. She was just hungry, waving her tail in long slow arcs, all sorrows passed.

In some strange way, Tom's were gone from him too. He fed her, then limped upstairs and stood for a long time in the shower.

He hadn't switched the tank on last night, and the water flowed cold, but he barely noticed. He dressed, paused for long enough to disinfect and plaster the worst of the cuts on his feet and his hands, then went out into the rain-washed morning. The wind was fresh, rich, full of salt. Opening the Land Rover's door, he stood for a moment, letting the air's damp turbulence rock him.

He was here. He was glad he'd booked the locum, but he was here, on his feet in the morning light, not dragging himself off the sofa with the black jaws of his hangover sunk deep inside him. Not crawling out of the pit.

Getting into the truck, he started her up and headed for the road. The rain increased, and he switched on her lights, watched the sweep of the windscreen wipers with a kind of peaceful satisfaction. Clear, he was clear. His mind stretched out like the headlamps, finding the path ahead. He knew, after years of *one drink won't hurt* and *I can deal with it*, that he was and always would be an addict, and that his only salvation—not his cure, never that—lay in absolute sobriety. He knew that he was locked in mourning for one lover, that his efforts to accept another, with this grief unaddressed in his heart, had been hopeless from the beginning.

He knew that he'd lost Flynn. Turning onto the lonely stretch that would take him past Lanyon on the road to the Hawke Lake base, Tom took firm hold of the wheel against the wind's buffeting, set a straight course. He'd lost Flynn, but, God, Flynn didn't have to *be* lost, not to the whole world, not to everything a man like that could have and do if he could be set free. Taking Tremaine from him, turning him in, was not the answer, even if Tom had been sure of his facts, and as time had gone by he was becoming increasingly uncertain. All he could do was tell Flynn what he thought, what he feared, and leave it up to him.

The quoit this morning had hidden itself entirely. Tom shook his head, trying to squint through the veils of the rain. No, there it was—crouching low, looking ready to run. He remembered hot light and warm hands on his bare skin, guiding his movements, opening him up. Pain went through him with a clarity that snatched his breath. God, not much hope for him in a bottle now anyway, was there? He'd drunk because he couldn't feel, and the numbness of a skinful was preferable to that dead zone inside. It was all restored to him, the full bloody human birthright—from the stinging ache in his cuts to the tearing, oddly physical sensation of loss in his heart. The piercing joy that lit him up in spite of everything, when he thought of Flynn.

Headlights in the road ahead. Couldn't be, Tom thought calmly, beginning to brake anyway. Too close, too fast, and on the wrong side. He started to pull over. The road curved round to the right here—not much escape for him, and the Rover's tyres were already bouncing and slipping on mud, but plenty of room on the far verge when the other driver saw him. There was a blind crest ahead. Tom, out of evasive manoeuvres, braced and hoped.

His serenity never wavered. He was thinking of Flynn when the vast truck roared over the crest, full beams blazing, all the way over on the left. Still somehow he was lit up inside, hauling the wheel round in the movement that would smash him into the wall.

No. A gap about four yards long, where the drystone had crumbled. The Rover shot off the road at fifty. Hit the barbed-wire fence that bridged the gap, which slowed her momentum a little but flipped her, turned her flight into a wild sideways arc. She hit turf and rocks on a diagonal, shattering windscreen and bodywork, rolled once and slammed down onto her driver-side flank.

Not much point in worrying about car wrecks, was there? The thought came to Tom slowly, as if wrapped in clouds. It became tangled up with a raw scent of petrol, a threatening darkness, and almost slipped away, but he snagged it back, interested in this new aspect on an old fear. He'd seen so many crash victims. Wondered how they'd felt—if a crippling terror had entered them, an anticipation so dreadful that impact must have come almost as release. Did he have his answer now? He wasn't sure of anything anymore, but maybe if you got that much time to think, you'd avoid the bloody crash in the first place. He hadn't had a second. The period between knowing it would happen and the whole thing being over was…

Nonexistent? One dark flash? His mind, on the run from its prison, tried to give him the right word, but there didn't seem to be one. He had felt something. A bang, like a roadside device going up, but inside him.

Thinking of these things, struggling to define them, was very tiring. He lay for a while in the rain. The wind was howling in the Rover's undercarriage, a mournful, familiar sound. He could hear a rhythmic creaking, like the spin of a disengaged tyre. A gentle pattering, cold small feet, on one side of his face, in the open palm of his hand. *Flynn*, he thought, with utter satisfaction, beginning to fall away.

He must have said it out loud.

"Yes. I'm here. Oh, holy fucking *Christ*, Tom. Hang on."

Another cloudy interval. When he surfaced again, it was to full inhabitation of his flesh, and all he could do was fight not to let go, not allow his ragged breathing to turn into the howls of pain and fear that had suddenly surged up inside his chest. The Rover was lying on her side on the moorland turf. He had gone through the windshield and was trapped from the thighs down in her crushed wheel housing. "Oh… God, Flynn…"

"Here, sweetheart. Breathe. Just breathe. Did this thing have no airbag? Weren't you wearing your belt?"

No, he tried to say to him. *No, too old a model. No, for the first time in my last neurotic, triple-checking, terrified three years, I drove off without it.* "See," he managed, smiling faintly. "This is what happens."

"Too bloody right. Gonna get help for you. Just hang on." The feel of a warm hand on his hair, brushing broken glass off his face. The click of a mobile being flipped open, then a triple beep, repeated two seconds later. A volley of swearing that almost made him laugh. Navy boys, no matter how civilised, were all the same underneath. "Godforsaken bastard of a country. Can't get a fucking signal."

"No. Not here. Go…" Tom's throat seized, and he clung to Flynn's hand through a spasm of coughing. "Back to the road. About fifty yards south. Parking bay. There's… There's a clear patch."

He was gone. Tom listened to the fading pounding of his footsteps on the turf, and wished he could see him. A lovely sight, he'd be willing to bet, that light-made frame at full pelt. The vision deflected his thoughts for a moment. Then he was cold and alone. Shock began to hit him. He felt the first jolts of his reaction, a convulsive shivering, and fought to stay still, to do all the things he would tell a crash victim to do. *Breathe. Don't struggle. Don't, for God's sake, start crying out after your saviour to forget the bloody phone call, to please come back and not let you die here alone.*

"All right. They're coming."

Tom released a pent-up breath, the one that had been holding back that last plea. The turf had resounded once more to running feet. There were warm hands on him. He swallowed hard, tasting blood. There was Flynn, kneeling on the grass outside the Rover's wrecked and empty windshield frame. Irrelevantly Tom noticed that he was wearing the grey T-shirt he had given him. That he was soaked to the skin, and fighting not to cry. "It's okay," he told him. "Be okay. Do I… Do I get a Sea King, then?"

"For this? You're joking. Common or garden ambulance, for you. And some firemen with the tin opener." It was a good effort. Tom heard it—Flynn sounded good. Giving him back at least his own effort at humour. On the blurry edge of his vision, Tom saw him lean to look through to the Rover's rear, which a glance in the cracked rearview had told him was a mangled hell of torn metal and vinyl. "Oh, God. Not Belle."

"No," Tom said. "No, she's at home." Now that he thought about it, there was something he needed to tell Flynn, wasn't there, about Sea Kings. It was why he'd been on the road in the first place. Something important…

"Tom. Tom! Wake up. You do not bloody drift off, you hear me?"

Struggling back at the harsh command, Tom became aware that Flynn was reaching past him to drag through from the back the tartan rug he carried for Belle. The one Tom had given him, he now remembered irrelevantly, to wrap around himself a million years ago at Porth beach. Flynn had been cold then, hadn't he? Bleeding as Tom was now, from dozens of places where his shirt was ripped and blossoming red in the rain. Tom felt barriers of perception and identity slide. His blood, or Flynn's? Flynn was bruised, he knew that much. Terrible livid thumbprints on his arms.

Covering his shoulders with the rug, Flynn said suddenly, as if following Tom's thoughts, "Tell me Rob did not do this to you."

"What?" The question called him back from a great and increasing distance. He was stupid, he supposed. It hadn't occurred to him. Wasn't occurring now. "No. Of course not. Wasn't his truck. Listen. I'm sorry, Flynn. What I said to you about him… Didn't mean to hurt you." That was it, though. Something about Tremaine, and the Sea Kings. *Don't fly with him.* He had to say it, but the shuddering was boiling up in him again, his body's hopeless reflex to tear itself out of the trap. "Flynn, don't—"

"No. Stay still." Flynn crouched low, reached over the wheel arch and grabbed him. "Got to stay still. Come on, Doc, you know this stuff. Ssh." Tom wondered if his face was intact. He hoped so. Flynn was kissing blood and rainwater off it, holding him down. "I've got you. Keep still." He stroked his hair, and Tom used a last access of strength to reach up for him. "That's it. Hang on to me."

A time passed. At first Tom listened for sirens, then he lost that thread and began to track the rhythmic warmth of Flynn's breath, coming and going against his cheek. So much had happened, hadn't it? This man's irruption into his life, an unexpected daybreak. Then night coming down again, so hard it had almost consumed him. And yet Flynn was here with him. The strangeness of that drifted over Tom's mind like cobwebs, or the dandelion fluff he could see catching on the wet cotton of Flynn's T-shirt. "How… How did you find me?"

A quiver of fraught laughter went through Flynn. "Oh, well… Remember how I bumped into you by chance at the quoit the other day? It only took me three goes. I reckoned it was worth another try."

"Oh great. My beautiful stalker. Did you…?"

"Tom. Hush a minute."

Tom fell silent. A new tension had seized the lean shoulders he was holding. Tom felt him inhale—took a diagnostic breath himself, of the sharpened petrol tang in the air. "What is it?"

"Not sure. I…" He paused, absolutely still. Listening. And Tom heard it too. A trickling sound, and then a soft and utterly unique thump. "All right. Got to get you out."

"Thought you said I had to stay still."

"That was then, sunbeam."

Tom waited. There was one last moment of uncertainty, terminated by the hiss of spilled fuel igniting. "Oh, you're kidding. A spark? In this bloody weather?"

"Yeah. Shit out of luck today, aren't you, Doc? Don't worry." Flynn braced his shoulder into the distorted shield frame and got a hand beneath the steering column. "Got to lift this a bit. Can you push?"

His contribution would be token at best, but he appreciated Flynn's effort to distract him. Then he understood why he had made it. "No. Flynn. Get out."

"In a minute."

"No. Now. The tank's gonna go up."

"Push up from under the wheel. Come *on*, Tom."

I filled her up yesterday. Full load; cost me a fortune. She'll blow like a culvert bomb. "Flynn, fuck off out of here," he rasped, trying to shove him away. But he was too weak, the pain occasioned by his movement too unmanning, and he fell back. Something in him still was capable of admiration, of aesthetic response—God, the sight of Flynn, every muscle in his lean tanned arms corded and standing, shoulders straining against the frame… *No, don't die here. You're too damn lovely.*

But he was tough as whipcord too? Flynn hauled deadweight bodies out of freezing water and into rescue baskets for a living. By contrast with a heaving Atlantic storm, Tom supposed the fire starting up in the back of the truck might not seem to him that much of a threat. He watched him lock a grip beneath the Rover's crushed dashboard, pulled until Tom thought he could hear ligaments tearing down his spine. Something in the wheel housing cracked. He got an inch, got a couple, and then it would do. Grabbed Tom by the armpits and dragged him out of the wreck.

They ran. Not far, but far enough. Tom knew a moment's wild elation. He was whole, his legs beneath him numb but working. He was running with Flynn, back on Porth beach, outrunning the ninth wave. When Flynn tackled him to the turf, it felt like brief flight, a cliff dive. He did not see or hear the truck explode, experienced the blast as a jolt through Flynn's body where it lay over his, a warm unflinching shield.

***

Days passed in flickering shadows. Their airless antiseptic heat was so familiar to Tom that he did not question it, and simply dreamed himself making his rounds in the ICU, dispassionately looking down on his own bruised flesh laid out on the hospital bed. He borrowed the voices of his colleagues, of Mike Findlay, making diagnosis, trying to reassure the dishevelled young RNAS airman sitting by his bed that he would live. *Don't worry. There was some swelling on his brain, some pressure, but it's coming down. He'll wake up soon.*

I should never have moved him.

If you hadn't, he'd be in more bits than that clapped-out truck of his. Is someone looking after his dog?

Yes. Victor Travers collected her and took her home.

You should go and get some rest. He really will be okay. Broken collarbone, bad bruising to his pelvis and legs. God knows how he got away with it. You saved his life.

I'd rather stay here, if I can.

A warm hand, closing around his. It opened a gate, let him back into himself, and he slept.

Many voices. Nearing surface, Tom began to reach for them, but his throat was numb, his limbs drugged and heavy. Some of them surprised him. Vic Travers, his Porth Bay burr breaking up into rough fragments. Then Florence: *Now, Victor! You heard what the doctor said. Don't you go upsetting yourself, or we'll have you poorly too, and he just got you better, didn't he?*

Mike Findlay, of course, talking to him as if it were an ordinary day, which was the right approach with coma patients. Tom approved, and flickered him a smile which made him exclaim and check the monitors. *Did you see that, Lieutenant? Not long now.*

Lieutenant… That meant Flynn. Flynn's voice flowed round him like sunlight. He waited for it, followed it. It rose and fell like the sun, arcing across his day. It told him ordinary things—that it was raining again, that Belle was eating Florence Travers out of house and home. It told him things that made his heart rate pick up, made him struggle to find his way back, striking up through the water. He had not known he could be loved. The warm hand gripped his. His waking skin felt the brush of a kiss to his cheek. *Come on, Tom. Please.*

The next time he heard the voice, the sunlight was gone from it. It was a flat black snap, a wolf's growl. *Rob, get out. I don't want you in here.*

Why? I'm here for your own good, lover-boy. You miss any more shifts, you're gonna get busted.

I'm taking leave. Seriously, Rob. I'll call security.

Nobody has this much leave. And I got you that job. Don't you dare piss it away.

I know everything you got me. I'll always be grateful.

A silence, deep enough to drown in.

But I love him, Rob. You have to let me go.

Chapter Eight
Storm

Summer gale, banging like fists off the window. A westerly, it would be heaping wave crests high off the peninsula, and something in this half-dream, half-vision broke Tom's trance, brought him bolt upright in the hospital bed, tearing drip lines from his arm and making the EKG squeal. Pain lanced through his shoulder, then through every other part of him, and he sat gasping, lost, staring at the night-black window where the storm roared and rattled the glass.

The door flew open, admitting Mike Findlay, his face set in a grim, life-saving mask Tom knew well. As he watched, it transitioned to a broad smile. "Ah, finally, your lordship." Stepping back, he shouted down the corridor, "It's okay. He's just unplugged himself. Right, you. Stay still and let me see to you."

"Why am I in here? Why am I not on the ward, like anybody...?" His throat seized. *Must've been intubated*, he thought, dazedly, gratefully swallowing the water Mike passed him. "...anybody else?"

"Coma patients depress people, especially if they're doctors. Bad advert for the NHS. We decided to hide you."

"Oh. Ta." Tom subsided against the pillows Mike had propped behind his back. "Coma patient, though? I wasn't..."

"No, you were just sound asleep for five days, scaring the crap out of everyone. You've had a stream of visitors, you know. And as for that poor lad from Hawke Lake..."

"Flynn? Is he all right? Where is he?"

"Don't begrudge him a night off." Mike finished listening to his chest and began shining diagnostic lights into his eyes. The room seemed full of people now—nurses turning down the sheet, checking the dressings on his legs, the tight strapping round his shoulder. "He's been here day in, day out. Couldn't get him to leave. Seemed to think you were in some kind of danger, though he wouldn't say what." Mike's eyes met his, bright with suppressed amusement. "Looks like you've got a friend there. About time, if you don't mind my saying so."

"Mike, shut up." Tom felt colour flood into his face—and then, just as quickly, felt it drain. "Weather sounds bad. Are the rescue choppers out?"

"Don't know. The lifeboat got a callout, I heard, and that other bloke from Hawke—Tremaine, is it?—came by to pick your Flynn up, so maybe they're expecting a bad night." Mike smiled. "You awkward bastard. Trust you to wake up now, after the poor sod sat here watching you sleep for five days."

I woke up because I heard the storm, and I was afraid.

***

Alone once more in his private room, Tom stared at the night-black glass, which gave him back only his own pale reflection. Five days on a drip had hollowed his face, put shadows under his eyes. A dragging weakness pulled at him. He knew how quickly coma patients lost muscle tone and was glad it hadn't been any longer.

He checked the bank of monitors beside the bed. He didn't seem to be hooked up to any of them anymore. Mike had taken the adhesive electrode pads from his chest, leaving pink circles. He had broken his collarbone, but cleanly, and it had been reset. When he sat forward, testing the elasticity of the bandaging round his shoulder and rib cage, he found that he was firmly held in place, and the pain, although startling, was bearable. He could function, would not pass out on the floor and lose this endeavour before he started it.

Not from that, anyway. Tom had somehow forgotten that he'd overturned his Land Rover at fifty and been dragged out from the wreckage. Before it exploded. Sitting on the edge of the bed, he buried his face in his hands. Flynn had stayed with him. Flynn would have stayed—through the blast and beyond. Parting unsteady fingers, Tom stared through them at the black-bruised strips of flesh which were as much of his thighs as he could see between the edge of his hospital gown and the place where the bandaging started. Dear God, Flynn would have stayed. Tom wasn't sure if his legs would take his weight, but there was nothing broken, and they had to. He had to get out.

Mike Findlay would stop him, if he knew. Tom reckoned he probably had ten minutes to make good his escape—he wouldn't be left any longer, not with that efficient soul on shift. Well, the benefit of working in a hospital was knowing its rhythms and side routes. Quickly, not letting himself think about what he was doing, Tom pushed himself upright and stumbled to the door.

The corridor was quiet. A silent barefoot crossing on the lino brought him to the fire stairs. Their concrete chill on the soles of his feet was a welcome distraction. Walking felt like struggling uphill through waist-high shale, and he clung to the banister, padding downward one step at a time. The gale battered its wings against the window here too, bringing with it a rattle of rain, reinforcing his purpose. In the locker room on the next floor down he had a change of clothes, a spare set he could fall back on in case of blood or vomit. A pair of running shoes too, he thought. A jacket he could wear to the gym or the pool. Yes, he could pull this off. He even kept a spare bloody cashpoint card in his locker, for what emergency he'd never been able to imagine, but he finally had reason to be glad of his neurosis-fuelled duplication of resources.

By the time he had crept into the locker room, got the clothes out of his locker and pulled them on over his bandages, he was about ready to fold up and weep with the pain. What the fuck was he doing? Flynn was probably fine. Rob had come to take him back to Hawke, that was all. They'd need him in one way or another, on a night like this. If Tom was that worried, all he had to do was find Mike and ask him for help.

Yes, right. *I need you to make sure Lieutenant Summers doesn't fall into the hands of his violent, possibly homicidal ex, on this night of black tempest. Explain to him. Extract him somehow from Rob Tremaine's brutal enchantment. Don't let him fly…*

A time passed, of walking and pain, of pain concealed in the best casual walk he could manage. He made his way out of the hospital via supply and admin corridors, deserted at this hour, and found himself swaying, grabbing at a wall for support, in the alley that ran behind the main block. The wind immediately caught him, rain stinging into his face. Running his hands across his hair, Tom straightened up and tried to look like an ordinary, unremarkable man, in search of a cashpoint in the Penzance streets. Ordinary men did such things—they ran out of cigarettes or booze and went out, even after midnight in a storm, to get some money and go to the off-licence or the promenade's one enterprising twenty-four-hour shop. Tom could be one of those men, no bother.

He made it to the Lloyds just off the seafront, then stopped a taxi disgorging a handful of revellers into the wind-whipped night. Bunny ears and tiny skirts… Tom had no idea what day it was, but assumed a Friday or Saturday. Good, the pub in Breagh would be making the most of its new extended licence. No point in trying to scale the walls of Hawke Lake. The bartender in the Fox, unobtrusive eyes and ears, would tell him what was going on. He got into the cab—a little too casually, the movement nearly made him faint—and he sat in clench-jawed silence for ten seconds before he was able to speak, the cabbie eyeing him warily in the rearview mirror. "Can you take me up to Breagh village, please?"

I love him, Rob.

Not a dream. Tom had learned, and taught younger doctors, that coma patients often retained hearing, and therefore to mind what they said at the bedside. Staring out through the rain-smeared glass, each speed bump and pothole sending high-voltage flashes of pain down his spine, Tom hung on to the door handle and smiled.

***

Half an hour later, he stood in the middle of the road outside the Fox in Breagh village. He was quite alone and unobserved. The pub had been near empty when he had paid the cabbie and stumbled in. Should have asked him to wait, he supposed, but he hadn't been thinking. The bartender, wearily mopping countertops, had told him that most of Hawke's personnel had been called back to the base on standby. They had one rescue chopper down with mechanical problems, the two others out already on separate emergency calls to fishing boats caught in this storm, which had roared up out of nowhere, barely registering on charts before it was ripping sky and sea to shreds. The ASaC lads had been called in too. The bartender supposed he shouldn't be telling Tom this, but there was word of a big trafficking run, arms dealers risking all to hide behind the storm and get a shipment through. A bad night, it was going to be. Would Tom like a drink before he closed the shop?

No. Absolute sobriety, forever. Tom remembered, in a weird flash, laying down that law for himself before leaving the house on a wet morning five days ago. Before the road, the mist, blazing headlights rearing up at him. He had not expected such challenge to come so soon. This was how it would be, to love a man like Flynn. A man who leapt into the storm, who would never be grounded or tamed. Never be safe... How fucking sweet it would be, to knock back a treble, buy the bottle, find his way home somehow and leave the night to take care of itself. No one would be any less dead or alive in the morning for his contribution.

Nevertheless he turned and walked away. As soon as he closed the pub door, the gale hit him, pushing him unresisting out into the deserted street. He heard a key turn in the lock behind him. He was soaked to the skin inside thirty seconds. As he stood swaying, trying not to drop to his knees on the tarmac, he heard the thud of rotor blades. He looked up. Briefly the night was lit by the flying-whale shape of a Sea King, a darkness on darkness, picked out by the red and green flicker of her running lights. Rescue or tactical? Tom couldn't tell. The sound of the spinning blades merged into the wind and was gone.

He turned, disoriented, at another engine's roar. Earthbound, this one, accompanied by a pair of flickering, unreliable headlights. Tom began to move towards the kerb, wondering if he would be quick enough. Each step now felt like dragging lead weights upstairs. He wondered who had run him off the Lanyon road.

Why the driver hadn't stopped, and if, as now seemed likely, he was coming back to have another go.

Tyres squealed on the wet road. Blinking, shading his eyes from the uncertain glare, Tom saw a battered Ford van pull up next to him. The door swung open and Victor Travers scrambled out. "Thomas bloody Penrose," he greeted him, grinning. "Thank God for that. Doc Findlay wanted to call out air-sea rescue, but they're all busy, so you got me. What the devil are you doing here?"

Tom didn't resist Victor's large and comprehensive grasp on him. The passenger seat of the Ford felt like a welcoming mattress. If he closed his eyes… "How… How did you know where to find me?"

"Didn't. This road's just on my beat. Your other friends and neighbours are out cross-quartering the rest of the countryside. Come on, let's get you back."

"Wait a second, Vic." Tom hesitated, distracted. Did he *have* friends and neighbours? Of the sort, anyway, who would turn out after midnight in a storm to find him? "Please. Don't drag me back to the hospital. Call Mike and tell him I'm safe, to call off the search, but…"

Victor eyed him. It occurred to Tom that his friend could be forgiven for jumping to a conclusion, finding him like this just after closing outside the only pub in a five-mile radius. But all Vic said was, "What's the matter? I know all the choppers are out tonight. You worried about Flynn?"

Tom flinched. Victor had been there when David Reay had died, but the difference in rank between them, and the fact that no one was meant to know, had prevented him from offering Tom a single word of comfort. Not military etiquette. Tom knew, to his shame, that he was still trammelled by some of it now. To hear Victor name Flynn as someone he might care about was hard.

"Look," Victor said harshly. "We're civilians now. And it's the twenty-first century—even in Cornwall. That lad sat by your bed round the clock, Tom. If you're not bloody worried about him, you should be."

A day of revelations. Tom sat listening to the storm rock the van. He could not work out if he had woken up into a new world or had unexpectedly learned to see the real nature of the old one. Friends and neighbours scouring the country for him. Mike Findlay's expression when he opened the door to find him awake. Victor, whom Tom had always thought of as the essence of British soldiery, blunt and tough, straight as a die, watching him now in a painful mix of annoyance and compassion.

"Yeah," he said, voice helplessly cracking on the word. "I am. But what do I do with it, Vic? He's out there, and I'm here. Grounded. What do I do?"

Victor sighed. "You promise me you're not gonna drop down dead on me if I don't take you back to Doc Findlay?" After a moment Tom nodded, meaning it as far as he could. "All right. The lifeboat's out. Florrie's making tea for the wives and other halves. Come down to Porth Bay with me. They'll show you what you do."

***

The RNLI station in Porth was brightly lit up, a brave neon box in the wild night. As Victor helped him out of the van on the harbourside, Tom saw that the waves were crashing almost to the top of the lifeboat's vacant launch ramp. "How long has she been out?"

"Nearly three hours now. We've lost radio contact with them. And there's nobody to back them up tonight."

No. Tom could see that it was not easy. He knew almost all of the dozen or so people gathered in the station office—by sight, at least, or as patients. He hadn't permitted himself anything else. Most of them looked tired, a few pale and sick, as if the three hours had been very long. They looked up as he and Victor entered. A few smiles of recognition, surprise. One or two nodded and greeted him by name. Florence Travers, busy with a tea urn in the corner, looked up and broke into a wide grin. "Tom! Thank God you're on your feet again."

Vic put a hand to his back. "You okay?"

"Yes. Just about."

"Good. Florrie, he's come to make himself useful."

She nodded, gave him a look of unsentimental understanding. "That's right. Better than sitting at home, isn't it?"

So Tom helped serve tea to the wives and other halves. What struck him—apart from his sense of utter unreality, handing over plastic cups, asking who wanted sugar, while the gale screamed so hard outside that the little concrete building seemed to rock—was that he was not the only man in the gathering. One of the others was a father, granted, widowed Bill Hughes whose only son was one of the lifeboat volunteers, but he could not account for Christopher Poldue, who as far as Tom had known lived a bachelor life in the flat above his antiques shop. Poldue was a standoffish type—but, then, to all appearances, so was he.

When next he limped past the plastic chair where Poldue was sitting, he paused. "It's Christopher, isn't it?" The other man nodded, and he cautiously sat beside him. "Got somebody out there?" he asked, half expecting to be told to mind his own business, but Poldue's expression suddenly altered, and he said quietly, "Yes. Gavin Wilkes. Do you know him?"

"Of course." Tom did. Wilkes taught at the village primary school in Tremethick Cross. He reflected that, while Vic might think it was the twenty-first century, Poldue and Wilkes must have had a hard time of it. No wonder he lived quietly. "God, Christopher," he heard himself saying, to his own surprise. "How do you stand it? Nights like this?"

Poldue regarded him with calm grey eyes. He looked very tired, but serene. "It's what they do. All you can do is accept it. Make the best of every second you can spend with them, and then…you let them fly."

***

Tom waited, doing his best to accept. He was not sure for how long. Desultory conversation rose and died, then dropped away with a cold finality when the beeping of someone's watch announced that the fourth hour was up. The Morvah postman's wife, heavily pregnant, broke into helpless tears and immediately began apologising for it. There was a code of behaviour, Tom had already gathered, to which everyone would adhere for as long as they could. But Florence went and put an arm around the girl. She looked across at Tom, who was unconsciously cracking a plastic cup to shreds between his hands. "It's all right, Evie. Been a long shift tonight, eh? And you're getting tired. Tom, why don't you come and have a look at her?"

In checking her pulse, laying a hand to her belly and gently joking with her about the chaos that would ensue with the arrival of her twins, Tom briefly lost his own concerns, and he supposed that this too was part of how the waiting was done.

He barely heard Vic's mobile beep, and was still crouching in front of Evie when he came back from the adjacent room. The phone was still open in his hand. "All right, everyone," he said. "Long Rock Point just heard from them. They waterlogged their radio, but your James remembered his torch Morse, Evie, and signalled to the lighthouse crew. It'll take a good two hours, but they're on their way home."

Tom stood back, out of the way of their celebrations. He thought that, if he switched the lights off, he would still be able to see them, each one haloed in the electricity of human joy. The air in the storm-rocked little room was ablaze. Christopher Poldue very stiffly and courteously kissed Evie, then to Tom's surprise turned to him and took his hand. "There. Good news, eh? Which one were you waiting for?"

"Me? Er… No one on the lifeboat. One of the air-sea rescue crew."

"Oh. That's harder still." He shook Tom's hand warmly. "Good luck, Dr. Penrose."

Tom thanked him, smiled as best he could and turned to go. Where, he wasn't sure. His just-woken brain kept trying to tell him he had a Land Rover parked somewhere nearby and could choose. The idea of his own empty home was repulsive to him. Back to the hospital, he supposed. His own reluctance to go there had to be secondary to Mike Findlay's anxiety and the amount of trouble Vic would get into for colluding in his escape. Vic was still standing in the doorway—maybe he would give him a lift.

"Tom," he said. "Come here a second." He drew him into the next room. "Listen. Florrie's sister works on the phones up at Hawke Lake. I gave her a ring to see if I could get some news about Flynn. She says the rescue chopper was forced down by high winds off Padstow. They're all okay, but…Flynn wasn't rostered on their shift tonight. She thinks he went out with the enforcement team on some weapons-trafficking op, and now they're out of contact too." He put out a hand to catch Tom's arm. "Here. Don't you pass out on me, Doc. Does that mean something to you? Is something going on?"

Tom leaned on the wall. It did not stop the nauseating heave of the room's floor beneath him, but it kept him upright. He had to do better than—or at least as well as—the pregnant girl waiting to hear she'd lost her husband. He said dryly, "I don't know for sure. Just…trouble. Christ, Vic! There's nobody to help them."

"Well, they've called the Devon and Exeter coastguards, but it'll take them a while to…" He tailed off, looking at Tom assessingly. "Doc. In your honest medical opinion, how are you?"

Tom frowned at the dead-serious note of the question. "What? I'm okay. Does it matter?"

"Believe me, it does."

"Well…" Bewildered, Tom tried to take a professional inward glance. "Nothing broken but my collarbone, and that's strapped. My legs are bruised and lacerated. Vitals are low, but that's because I've been on a drip-feed for five days, apart from Florrie's biscuits."

"Functional, then?"

"Just about."

"Right. Come with me."

***

Tom stood in Vic Travers' boathouse, his sense of unreality increasing by the second. The building was the size of a light-aircraft hangar. At one time, he remembered, Vic's father had employed half of Porth Harbour in here. The smell of paint and pitch, and the dim light from the few remaining bulbs, hung solemnly in the air, a stillness made deeper by the roar of the storm outside.

Only three of the twelve building berths were occupied. Two looked like simple jobs, such as he'd known had been all poor Vic was capable of on his return from his last tour of duty. He recognised the upturned hull of the Reeves' fishing smack, getting her seams recaulked, and a canoe Vic had told him he was making for his nephew's birthday. The third berth's occupant was much larger and cloaked in a massive tarpaulin that Vic was now briskly unbuckling and pulling back.

"Here," he said. "I've had to keep her wrapped. You know how Florrie talks, and I wasn't sure if I'd ever get her finished. But apart from her colours, she is."

The boat was a replica, down to the last measurement, of the RNLI lifeboat that had gone out on its mission that night. However, unlike that well-used lady, her paint was glossy and intact, her powerful lines unbroken by wear and tear. Further, as Vic smilingly explained, helping Tom down off the berth side and onto her deck, she had a one hundred and fifty horsepower Mercury outboard motor twice the size of the current boat's, a top speed of forty knots, and state-of-the-art radar.

Tom looked around him wonderingly. "God almighty, Vic. Did they commission you?"

"No. I'm sure I was meant to spend my army payout on food for the kiddies and visits to the shrink, but this seemed better." He crouched by the motor housing and gave the starter a brief, expert yank. Immediately a purring roar filled the boathouse. Belatedly Tom realised that this berth, with its ramp and double doors at the end, was for launching.

Vic straightened, grinning. "Lived here all my life, Doc!" he yelled over the noise. "Watched the lifeboats going in and out, bringing people home. This is my contribution. She's called the *Shell shock*. I'm gonna donate her, if we don't sink the bitch tonight."

Tom looked at him. For a moment, the gale found a voice even louder than the throbbing Mercury, but he did not hear it. He was feeling the beginnings of a bright, prickling heat, in his chest and his belly, at once strange and utterly familiar. The pain in his limbs seemed to drop from him. Yes, he remembered this. It was the pure joy of action, most of it lost back in boyhood, the dregs of it spilled out across the dust of Afghanistan. Of not thinking but *doing*. He said, "I'll get the doors."

"You'll wait a bloody second," Vic corrected him. He opened a locker in the cabin and handed Tom a life vest. When he looked up from fastening it, his friend was holding out to him what he took for one second to be a flare gun—then recognised for a Browning 9mm service revolver, from the weight of it loaded and ready.

"Vic… What the fuck?"

"There's something not right about Bobby Tremaine, isn't there? That's why you're so worried."

Bobby Tremaine. You know him too. Tom swallowed dryly. "Yeah. I'm not sure whose side he's on. And he's got Flynn."

"Right. So whatever he's up to, I doubt we're gonna *talk* him out of it. Take the gun. I know you can shoot—can you operate radar and navigate?"

In helicopters, military convoy planes when he was doubling up for injured crew. The principle was, he prayed, the same on water. "Just about. Yes."

"Good lad. I'll pilot. Their last point of contact was ten miles out from Trewellard. We can be there in half an hour."

Chapter Nine
The Ninth Wave

Forty-five degrees of pitch and yaw—up, down, port or starboard. Tom knew that, had his whole focus not lain thirty miles ahead of the boat, he would have lapsed into seasick terror within five minutes of launch. He had been out on some wild nights, but never with a maniac like Vic, riding sole shotgun on a craft that really required a six-man crew to keep her stable and operational.

The first few jolts from wave crest to trough went through his spine like a pile driver. And *shotgun* was generous—Vic's top-line replica had her navigator and GPS station out front in the prow, while the pilot manned the wheel from behind his right shoulder. The sense of being catapulted forward from the rear increased the sense of helplessness, absolute lack of control, to a pitch that would have done for Tom before the advent of Flynn into his world had set the whole thing flying off its axis anyway.

And if he had to be shot blindly into the dark, who better to trust with the task than Vic? Shell-shocked nutcase he might be, but centuries of wrestling the ocean ran in his blood. Tom soon saw a pattern to his madness, began to pick up how he raced the lifeboat in zigzag lines from crest to crest, angling her back and forth to increase speed and lessen the swell's drag on the hull. No one could have driven her faster. Knowing this—watching the lights of Porth Bay recede on either side of him—a great elation seized Tom, so warm and bright it felt like inner wings unfurling, felt as if it would crack his ribs from the inside. They were going out to find Flynn. The next wave which burst up over the prow soaked him to the skin, and his own laughter joined with Vic's wild roar of amusement. All fear died. He had one task. He turned his attention to the GPS and radar and hung on.

They were at the Trewellard coordinates within twenty-five minutes of launch. Victor eased off the engine when they drew near to target, allowing Tom the time and steady deck he needed to make a thorough radar sweep. A downed chopper would show up fine, but Tom knew—thought Victor did too—that they were not searching for an intact craft in the water. Not by now. If the SAR helicopter had been afloat, they would have signalled home. All they could hope for was wreckage.

Inside himself, Tom was running another countdown too. Half an hour since last contact. A bailed-out crew would be nearing the end of the time they could expect to survive in Atlantic water in June. The rules were fairly strict. People usually followed them, with the exception of the occasional child who dropped into a deathlike hypothermia and came back like Lazarus when warmed up hours later.

Victor yelled his name over the wind, calling him back from a chilly distraction. "We should be right on top of them. Anything?"

"Not a bloody thing." Not looking up from the screen, Tom felt Victor lock the helm and come to stand beside him. Without her forward momentum, the boat was a cork on the waves. Slap after drenching, blinding slap of salt water cracked against her hull, exploding spray into his face and across the instrumentation.

"Look, Vic," he said hoarsely, dragging a cloth across the panel for the fiftieth time. "Nothing. Christ, they must have gone under."

Victor didn't reply. He reached across Tom, steadying both of them with his grip on the rail, shielding him from some of the gale's ferocity while Tom reset the unit and began another sweep. "No, wait. There. Look!"

"Okay, yes. That size, though, could be a porpoise or a fish school."

Tom understood. Victor, the good soldier, would offer neither empty words of comfort nor of hope, not until they were sure. He swung away from the radar, and a moment later Tom heard the engines snarl as he turned her in the direction of the screen's pale ghost.

The rigid-inflatable life raft, low in the water from the weight of her crew. The lights of the *Shellshock* picked out her RNAS colours and insignia, a match for her mother-ship chopper, as she became more than an echo on the scanner, and Victor steered close, bringing her round in a sweeping arc to protect her from the swell.

Tom remained at his station. The navigator's job was done, he supposed. In a moment, he would get up and help Vic throw out a cable, make sure it was caught, and haul the raft, with its waving, gesticulating cargo of lives, towards the relative safety of the larger craft. He would overcome the aching lassitude that had slowed his heartbeat, weighted his limbs with cold lead. He could not see Flynn, in the strobing, shifting light. The faces of the rescued men were sombre, even while they yelled their greetings and thanks across the diminishing gap. Tom knew the look, from a hundred returned mission-flights into Bastion—they had lost someone.

The sight of Victor fighting to unhitch the heavy tow-cable brought him round. Mechanically he shoved himself upright, the pain he had forgotten boiling up from his legs and broken ribs. Two of the ASaC crew, soaked and shivering in their flight suits, were reaching out, the others moving automatically to balance the raft's far side. Tom went to join Vic, and between them they rolled out enough of the wire that the survivors could grab it, locking it tight to the RIB's rail. There was more to be done. Tom took it on himself, a last buffer between now and the moment when he would have to speak, to ask. Hitching the two boats together on one wire would soon damage both as the waves slammed them together, and he struggled against the *Shellshock's* pitch to secure the stern too, lashing both craft to one movement on the swell.

"Tom Penrose? Is that you?"

He jerked his head up. A third ASaC man had made his way to the back of the raft and was helping him, pulling the tow through his numb hands. Tom's cognitive process came slowly, but at last he recognised him—Charlie Mitchell, who regularly brought one or another of his increasing brood of kids to the surgery. He opened his mouth to answer him, but the cold seemed to have entered his throat and lungs, and he could only nod. "What are you doing out here, Doc? Is that Vic Travers? God… What's happened to the RNLI lads?"

Tom tried to put the question together with his reason for asking it, but Victor came to his rescue. "We're not the lifeboat, mate. A poor substitute, but at least we've got you. Or most of you, anyway. Where's…"

"Flynn," Tom broke in, finding his voice at last. He could not let Vic ask it. "Flynn Summers. Is he—?"

"They're gone. Him and Rob Tremaine. Dunno what the hell's been going on all night. We… Christ almighty!"

Tom reached to grab him. He held him fast as a huge wave smashed across both boats. It swamped the smaller life raft, knocking one of the surviving crewmen casually overboard. Tom waited till the water's fury was spent, and he had seen the others begin to haul their comrade back to safety, then he rasped, "Victor, help me get them on board here. Quick."

The transfer took less than a minute. Tom saw blood, black in the *Shellshock's* lights, and knelt instinctively beside the rescued crewman, beginning to examine his head wound. He was on autopilot. Behind him he could hear Charlie Mitchell continuing his story, in a shout over the wind, but he could not care. "We don't even know what Flynn was doing flying her. He hasn't logged a flight hour in two years. But our skipper—Tremaine—said there was nobody else. And he flew like a fucking angel, give him that. Got us out here so fast…"

"You were after the gun runners?" That was Victor, pulling poor shocked Mitchell back on track. Still Tom could not listen. He had nothing to treat this head wound with, but digging in one pocket, found a handkerchief—clean, of course, and scrupulously folded—and shook it out.

"No such thing as covert ops in bloody Cornwall, is there?" Briggs laughed unsteadily. "Yeah. Massive shipment. We were right above the coordinates, and suddenly Flynn tells us to bail. That he's dropping the raft for us, and not to ask questions. I tried to see through into the cockpit, and…it was chaos. Rob Tremaine was out of his seat. I thought he had a gun in his hand, for God's sake. I shouted through to him, to try to check the bail-out order, but it was like he didn't hear. So I…I took my men, like Flynn had told me, and we bailed. I was last out. Christ. Last second before we jumped, I think I heard a shot."

Tom turned around. He said to his patient, "Hold that in place until it stops bleeding." He lurched to his feet and turned to face Mitchell. *A shot.* His world was darkening, closing to a tight black tunnel around Briggs's last word. "Charlie. What happened to the helicopter?"

"She went down. I didn't see—too busy swimming for the boat—but Jim said she didn't just drop. Flynn can't have bailed. Someone took her into the water like a real pro."

"She didn't crash?"

"No. But there's no way she could've stayed afloat. And even if Flynn and Rob got out—"

Screw Rob. Tom was grateful for the seizure in his throat that kept that thought silent from Tremaine's ASaC crew. He swung round to find Victor—who was one step ahead of him, already beginning to unlash the RIB from the lifeboat. "You lads keep this," Victor yelled over his shoulder. "We'll take the raft. Start making for shore before the storm gets any worse. You can radio for help, but it's gonna be a while getting to you."

"What?" Mitchell took a step towards Victor, but Tom intercepted him, putting him quietly out of his path to the other cable. "We're not leaving you."

"We'll be okay. She's manoeuvrable, and she's got a good outboard. This one's more likely to stay afloat with the six of you aboard." Victor put out a hand, and Tom grabbed it, making what he knew was a poor leap for the raft and landing awkwardly, dragging himself immediately upright. "Get home!" Vic shouted, casting off. "Tell Hawke Lake we're looking for your pilots. Go on!"

***

The RIB was matchwood on the swell, more fragile even than the lifeboat, but Tom was almost past feeling her lurches and leaps. He was almost past feeling. He knew that Victor was making the best of a bad job at the rudder, revving stolidly from crest to crest. He knew that they were systematically quartering the area in which the chopper must have gone down. He was clinging to the life raft's searchlight rack, directing its solitary beam into the night with numb hands. Beyond the borders of these thoughts, there was nothing. *Flynn*, his mind said to him sporadically, each time bringing a flash of memory. A presence at his bedside in the hospital. Hitting the turf by the Lanyon road, the air leaving his lungs at the impact of another body on his. Of flesh that would immolate itself to shield him.

Flynn, in the rain, holding him out of the wreckage as his petrol tank caught fire. "Flynn," he said aloud, unable to tell if the bitter salt taste in his mouth was seawater or tears. Once more, like a prayer, swiping his eyes clear with his sleeve. "Flynn…"

Another flash—this one in the world with him, here and now. Orange on indigo black—one glimpse, in a trough between two heaving waves. For a nightmare second Tom could not get air into his lungs to yell to Victor, then it came, abrading, scalding. "Vic! Vic, come about!" Vic turned to him, face an expectant blank, waiting for a direction, some degrees or an *o'clock*, but Tom's brain would not supply him with such detail and he could only swing the searchlight round, throwing out its beam in silent gesture. "There!"

A buoy, or a fragment of wreckage. These possibilities rose up, frail shields, across the fire of hope. There was a third one too. Tom swore inwardly, to a god he had lost under the Afghan sun and rediscovered in the wreck of a Land Rover six days before, that he would not leave Rob Tremaine to drown. More specifically, that he would not reach out, cut the cords of his lifejacket, put a hand to the top of his head and shove him under to make sure. That he would not allow Vic, who had fewer scruples and had never taken a *do no harm* oath, to do it for him.

The RIB clambered, motor roaring, to the top of the next wave, and there it was again. No, not wreckage. A human shape. *Flynn.*

He was blue to the lips, his face serene. The seawater cradled him. Tom could not know when he had stopped fighting it—saw, in a kind of streaking slow-motion as he reached out with Vic over the side of the raft, that his watch had stopped, blurred with water and steam. But it had been half an hour when they had found the ASaC crew. Flynn had been in the water too long.

Too long for life to be flickering still behind his peaceful mask. Everything Tom knew—about the sea, about human biology—screamed out against it, and he thought, hauling the poor lost deadweight into the lee of the raft, that he understood. Accepted. His own heart was drowned inside him and it could not make a difference. His fists closed alongside Victor's in Flynn's soaked flight suit. Together they dragged him far enough out of the water for Tom to get hold of his belt. The sea, remorseless, even now not sated with what it had taken, heaped itself up more and broke across them all, nearly sending the RIB under. Tom sobbed, choking, heaving Flynn halfway on board over the gunwale tube, and Flynn beneath his hands gave one enormous twitch and began to fight like a wildcat.

He was trying to finish a conflict whose beginnings Tom struggled to imagine, as he and Victor pulled him in and pinned him down on the life raft's soaking deck. He was too waterlogged to get out more than a faint, rasped *Rob*, but the punch he threw was well aimed and sincere. Tom caught his fist. "Flynn. Flynn, love, it's me."

"Rob… *Bastard*, let me *go*…"

"Hush. Easy." Tom heard his own voice, the shudder of laughter in it, the raw edge of tears. "Flynn, for God's sake, it's Tom."

Flynn fought out of his grasp, evading Victor's too, and bolted upright. The move threw him into Tom's arms. Tom seized him tight, ignoring the convulsion that went through him. He wrapped one hand around the back of his skull. His hair was tangled and rimed with salt.

"It's Tom," he repeated, in a whisper against his ear, sealing the promise with a rough, clumsy kiss, rocking him. "I found you. Flynn, sweetheart. I found you. It's me."

Flynn went still. He stopped trying to tear himself out of Tom's embrace. Tom felt his two fists, which had been balled against his shoulders, open suddenly up. Felt against his neck, indescribably, the astonished waking gape of Flynn's mouth. The hands moved—reading him quickly like Braille, sweeping his shoulders, his hair. "Tom."

"Yes. You're okay."

"No. I must've died," Flynn stated calmly. Tom fought laughter. He sounded so sure of himself, and unfazed, as if death, even his own, was just another aspect of rescue work to be dealt with. "That, or I've got the cold-crazies, because…"

"I'm sure you do have those." The raft lurched, taking on another rush of water. Peripherally Tom saw Victor push upright and go aft. A moment later the outboard snarled, pushing them forward against the swell. He kissed the side of Flynn's brow. "But you're alive. Going home."

"No. Because you just see what you want." He paused, gasping, and Tom listened in concern to the half-drowned rattle in his chest. He struggled back a little, far enough to look into Tom's face, his eyes' sea-green burning eerily. "You just hear and you see what you want. Tom's in hospital. Findlay said he'd be all right, or I'd never have left him." He frowned, putting up an unsteady hand to brush Tom's face. "I'd never have left you. Oh, Christ. *Tom.*"

"That's right," Tom said in relief, as the hypothermic body he held shuddered back to reality, at the same time registering at last how much water it had swallowed and inhaled. Flynn sucked a noisy breath and began to cough. "That's right, come here. Sit forward." Tom pulled him up onto his hands and knees, held him tight against the boat's movement and his own expulsive spasms. When he could spare a hand, he tore off his jacket. It was soaked, next to useless, but on top of Flynn's flight suit would give him at least one layer of protection against the remorseless, leaching wind. He wrapped it round his shoulders, and saw that Victor was shrugging out of his oilskin. "Ta, Vic." He caught it as Victor threw it, and bundled that around Flynn too. "Okay, sunbeam. You done there? Your lungs clear?"

Flynn moaned. "Ought to be," he managed, on a faint wry rasp between fits of coughing and retching. "Be okay, Tom. Core temp's still over ninety. Organs are functional."

"Oh, an expert patient. I love those. Come on." He hauled him upright, aware of his own pain now only as background noise, a distant music he didn't need to hear. "Your bloody organs won't function much longer if they stay out here. Victor! You okay there?"

"Fine. Get him into the canopy. I'll take us home."

"Okay." He paused, glancing at Flynn, who was on his feet but barely conscious, eyes fluttering closed. "Vic. Keep an eye out for…the other one."

A vulpine grin lit Victor's face. "Yeah. I'll be sure to do that."

"I mean it. We have to." All kinds of reasons. The least of them was Tom's oath, or the manslaughter by neglect a failure to search would amount to. Tom remembered a dream, in which Flynn had sat by his hospital bed and dismissed Rob Tremaine for a reason that made his heart heave with painful joy even now, but he couldn't be sure. Not of what had happened, not what Flynn really needed. *We have to try, for Flynn's sake.*

Tom got him under the life raft's fabric canopy. It was a frail shelter, but the cessation of the wind, the minute easing of the sea's unending roar, felt like a shadow of paradise, which Flynn completed for him on the instant, struggling up from the deck and into his arms. He caught him. "Flynn, love!"

"How did you… How did you find me? How are you here?"

"Ssh," Tom advised him, smiling into his hair. He didn't have a lot of body heat to give him, but he wrapped both arms around him, gasping in relief when, after a moment's paralysed stillness, Flynn returned the embrace, bruisingly, frantic, around his ribs. Shivers were beginning to rack him—a good sign, a return to life. "Just breathe, all right? Hold on to me and get warm."

"How the hell are you and Vic Travers on my ASaC raft?" He seemed to hear himself and got his head up. "Tom. God. My crew."

"They're fine. All safe—Charlie Mitchell and five others." Tom said it to him straightaway and firmly, biting back a small sting of amusement. *My raft. My crew.* He did not know what had happened to Flynn tonight, but, even nine-tenths drowned, he was subtly altered. Tom sensed it like clouds burning off from the face of the sun. No, not altered—restored. A pilot, a leader of men. "You got them out."

"You've seen them? How? Tom, how are you here? You were so badly hurt. You wouldn't wake up."

"I'm okay. I did wake up. I think it was the sound of the storm. Mike Findlay said Rob had come to get you. I was afraid. I…I didn't want you flying with him. I went looking for you, but I found Vic instead. We heard Hawke Lake had lost contact with your team, and Vic brought me out here." He smiled, shook his head. "In his new home-built lifeboat, if you'll believe that. We came across your lads in the raft, and we swapped, so me and Vic could go on and search for you and…"

"And Rob."

"Yes." The clouds could return. Tom saw them gather in Flynn's eyes. His gaze became unreadable, pupils dilating in shock. "We're still looking, love. But if he went into the water the same time you did…"

"Yes." Flynn swallowed. "Yes. Before. He jumped, after—after I dropped the others. He couldn't have made it to the raft."

"Then…"

"He's gone." The words fell out toneless, stones into still water.

"I don't know. Vic's gonna radio for help as soon as a search chopper makes it down from Devon or Exeter. But… Ah, Flynn. I'm sorry. I don't hold out much hope."

Flynn stared into the canopy's shadows. His grip on Tom's waist slackened. Then he said, so faintly that Tom could barely pick out his words from the sea roar, "Thank God."

"What?"

"If he's dead—oh, thank God. Thank God."

He wept in silence. It took him a long time to wear himself out, and Tom, silent too, maintained a steadfast grip on him, staring unseeing over his shoulder. He was distantly aware that the storm beyond the life raft's shelter began at last to abate, that the endless night was giving way, a thin dawn light gathering through the canopy. He pressed his mouth to Flynn's skull, reading, as clearly as if he could see his thoughts, the war of shock, relief and sorrow being waged inside him.

When at last the heave of his ribs became less anguished, more a search for air, Tom eased him back a bit, letting him breathe. "Flynn… What happened tonight?"

Flynn coughed. He got his head up a little. "Oh, Tom," he managed, his voice worn to rags. "How could I have believed him? How did I stay under so long? I feel like—I feel like I just woke up."

"How did he get you to fly with him? Mitchell said he had a gun."

"Oh, it wasn't at gunpoint." He sat up, and Tom, looking at him in pained amusement, wished that either of them had a dry bit of cloth between them to wipe his face. He undid a button or two at the bottom of his untucked shirt, and did the best he could with that until Flynn caught up and gently batted his hand away, shuddering with mortified laughter. "Stop that, you idiot. No. I went voluntarily. Two of the ASaC pilots are laid up after a raid at Lowestoft, and…he said there was nobody else."

"Nobody else to fly?"

"Yeah. Yes. I said I'd go as his cable man, but not that. And he told me—how many lives I'd have on my conscience if I didn't. The kids in fucking Basra who would end up buying the guns getting smuggled through tonight, if we didn't stop them." Flynn paused, lifting a hand to his mouth. "He reminded me about the men I'd already killed, back in Portsmouth when I ditched the Lynx. Asked me if I remembered their names. He said it was a chance to put it right."

"Jesus, Flynn."

"No. Don't." Flynn grabbed the hand Tom had been lifting, in shocked affection, to his face. "Let me tell you. Please. Something happened. I have to tell you. I remembered…"

He fell silent for so long that Tom realised he was becoming lost in the recall, and gently prompted, "Something about last time you flew. The crash."

"Yes. Oh, God, you were right. It was something about lifting off, being in the pilot's seat again. Getting a Lynx off the pad—

like making a cow fly—or seeing the lights drop down and away, or—rain on the cockpit glass. For a while I didn't think I could do it, and then something clicked. Everything I loved about it before. Finding that place in the wind—I mean, they can train you and train you, but one day you find it by the seat of your pants, that…niche, that sweet spot where she'll ride the gale for you and not get torn to shreds."

Tom smiled, nodding. He would never need ask Flynn what his concept of God or religion might be. Even now, shaking with the remnants of near-fatal hypothermic shock, his face was rapt, the light of mystical experience filling his eyes. "Flyboy," he said, affectionately. "Pure bloody flyboy. What did you remember?"

"The prep room at Portsmouth, two years ago. Strapping on Kevlar, loading up a semiautomatic. Feeling—different, free, because I'd told him…I'd told Rob that afternoon I didn't want us to be lovers anymore. He was crushing the life out of me, Tom. Thought he owned me. Didn't know the meaning of *no*—I had to fight him like a fucking cougar if I wasn't in the mood. Though…" His voice scraped, and he tailed off, "Though I *did* fight him off then. I was a different man."

"No. The same man, just—undamaged. What happened next?"

Flynn flashed a glance at him, a smile of gratitude for the cue. "He went up as my copilot. Dear *God*, Tom—he must have had a deal with them, some fucking devil's bargain with the bastards we were after. I wonder—if I hadn't dumped him, was he gonna try and cut me in on it?"

"Maybe." Tom brushed his fringe back, kissed his brow. "Just think—you could've bought a real car."

Flynn snorted. "Shut up. I love my crappy toy Mazda."

"Yes. Me too. Go on. What happened?"

"Okay. It was so weird, like living in two time zones at once. Tom, he *sabotaged* that Lynx. He was quiet all the way out, and before we got into position he just got up, ripped his headset off, walked to the back of the cockpit and…cut the fuel lines. I've dreamed it over and over—seeing him pull the cover off the bulkhead, seeing his wire cutters flash. I didn't know it was a memory. We dropped like a stone. I shouted through to the crew in the back, but it was too late—for everyone but him, because he jumped half a second before we started to dive. He was ready."

"God almighty. And yet…he came back for you. That part's true."

"Yes. He came back." Flynn drew a shuddery breath and pressed a little closer to Tom. "I don't know why he risked it. I'm not sure… I'm not sure my life would have been worth a day's purchase, if I hadn't woken up without a single memory in my head from the whole fucking thing, except for the ones he sat by my bed and implanted, day after day. He told me I'd lost control of her. He was kind, when everyone else around me could barely bloody look at me, no matter how hard they tried. Even the doctors. He was there every time I opened my eyes. He said he would look after me."

Tom kissed his brow. "All right." Gently he wiped away the fresh tears with the pad of one thumb. "I'm guessing that's when he came into his family fortune."

"Mm-hm." Flynn nodded, making a dreadful attempt at a smile. "That's when four-by-fours and private doctors started to rain down from heaven. I suppose they made it worth his while. He'd never mentioned his family to me before then, but suddenly there they were. Knightsbridge Tremaines, and old money."

"Flynn, do you know who he really is? I mean, where he comes from?"

"Yeah, of course. Just like you did, thirty seconds after you met him. Three people told me he was Bobby Tremaine from the Sankerris council estate during the first week I was here. God, Tom—did he think I was going to judge him? My dad's an electrician from Derby. I know what it's like, being officer class in the Navy, if you're not descended from the bloody admiralty."

"Why did you let him carry on lying to you?"

"I don't know. He was really cagey about it. I suppose he was worried I'd ask him about the money, but I wasn't likely to do that, was I? I'd been quietly taking it for far too long. I was ashamed. I even passed his lies on to you, though I was pretty sure you'd recognised him too."

"Flynn, love, surely you've worked out by now you've got nothing to be ashamed of?"

"I don't know. When I think about that night off Portsmouth—knowing I didn't kill all those men, all our friends, by some stupid pilot error—I feel like my heart's going to explode with relief, even though none of them are any less dead because it wasn't my fault. And yet when I look back over two whole years, dormant, hypnotised, eating out of Rob's bloody hand, letting him—own me, screw me… Learning to like getting beaten down and fucked, because that was what I deserved."

"Flynn…" Tom shook his head, briefly unable to bear it. He lifted a hand to cover Flynn's mouth—felt its palm kissed, his wrist seized, as if Flynn too wanted to be silenced. Stopped. They watched one another mutely for a long while. Then Tom said, turning his hold to a caress, fingertips over Flynn's salt-blistered lips, "He tried it again, didn't he? Tonight?"

"How… How could he leave me to think it was my fault?" Flynn whispered. His face was white with anguish, as if he had only just realised for himself the enormity of it. "He must have known I was living in hell."

Because he was an evil fuck, Tom thought succinctly, but kept it quiet. Perhaps the loss of him, with all his faults, was too fresh to Flynn for him to be able to withstand much condemnation from anyone else. "I don't know," he said. "But—ultimately, everything he did was to keep you close to him. He risked his whole game to spare your life."

Flynn snorted. The sound of it warmed Tom's heart with its vigour, its ordinary derision—told him that Flynn would get over Rob Tremaine, and maybe the process wouldn't take long. "Not tonight, he bloody didn't. He shot out my collective. He just went and stood by the hatch and took aim. It was seeing him get up and walk away that finally broke down the memory block. I thought he was gonna put a bullet in me, and…I just didn't care. Then he jumped."

"Charlie Mitchell says you made a textbook job of putting her down."

"Mitch said that?" Uncomplicated pleasure lit Flynn's face, an airman's pride in his work. "I could, Tom. I could do that, take her down nice, and do my evac like I was in the training pool at Hawke, because I knew, I was fairly sure, that they'd all got out in time. They lived, so I could live too. And—I *wanted* to. For the first time in years. All I could think about was how much I wanted to see you again." He shivered, shook his head. "I can't believe you came out to find me."

Tom swallowed hard. "I'll always find you, love."

***

The storm was almost spent. Tom, on his knees, held Flynn's face with desperate tenderness between both his hands—kissed him and kissed him, as the motion of the swell beneath the raft lost its rage, became a rocking. Tears forced themselves from beneath his closed eyelids, stinging the windburn and healing cuts on his face. Flynn's arms were passionately laced around his neck, his face tipped up as if to the sun. When at last Tom couldn't breathe and stars were bursting over his dark field of vision, he broke away. "Stop," he rasped, chuckling. "I have to go check on poor Victor."

Flynn nodded. He was smiling dazedly. When Tom let him go, he subsided against the life raft's hull. "Okay," he said, putting up a hand to shield an enormous yawn. "If you need me to take a spell at the rudder…"

"Oh, yeah," Tom said, leaning over him to check the pulse at his throat. It was strong, but too fast, his system revving in its struggle to evict the deadly cold. Tom wrapped Victor's waterproof tightly around him. "We'll be sure to do that. You just stay curled up there. Keep breathing. Try and get some sleep."

When Tom stumbled out into the light, he found Victor quietly plying the raft through a new world. The storm, with Cornish thoroughness, had given way to a dawn whose shades of rose and delicate green denied that its fury had ever existed or been unleashed along this coast to the peril of so many lives. Far off to the south, Tom could see the weird architecture of the Morvah cliffs, blades and pinnacles catching the first rays of sun. His watchtower was almost visible from here. He tried to remember when he had left it, and remembered with a shock that it had been a week ago, in another different world.

"Vic," he said, and saw Victor, who had tranquilly been watching the skyline, turn and smile at him. "I seem to remember somebody saying you were looking after my dog."

"Yeah. You can have her back any time. She eats more than my three kids combined."

"I know." He came to settle cautiously on the gunwale tube, every inch of him protesting. "I'll settle up with you."

"Don't be daft. I owe you a lot more than a few tins of dog food." Vic glanced back at the canopy. "How's your flotsam?"

"Cold. Shocky. He'll be okay, though. Can I take this while you rest? With Flynn, if you don't mind—he needs the hypothermia-hug."

"Bloody hell, Doc. I think I'll leave that kind of thing to you." Vic's face lit up with a smile in which there was so much good-natured amusement, and such an absence of malice, that Tom heard himself break into laughter. "Nah, I'm fine here. We're nearly home. I radioed Porth to see if anyone could come and pick him up, but they're still pretty busy out there. Lots of damage. No casualties, though, apart from…"

"Tremaine. Yeah."

"What the hell happened?"

Tom released a breath. He could hardly believe himself, in the sweet morning air, the rupture that had racked the night. "Sounds like he was getting paid to stop the ASaC lads from getting to that arms shipment. He brought their Lynx down to make sure."

"Christ almighty." Suddenly Victor raised his head, frowning at the western horizon. Tom followed his gaze. His ears were still ringing with the roar of the storm, but he could discern—faint, growing stronger every second—the song of another boat's engine. Vic shrugged, shook his head. "Typical, that is. Too little, too late."

"Is it the lifeboat?"

Victor shielded his eyes. "Doesn't sound like her." He squinted off across the water. "No, it's a launch of some kind. Sunseeker, I think. I don't recognise her. Suppose they might've sent someone from Hawke."

Tom nodded. He was getting a bit sleepy, his body wanting to shut down and attend to its damage. A fast launch from Hawke, or even passing tourists or fishermen, would be good—they could take Flynn off, get him to hospital, not that Tom could imagine letting him out of his sight. "We should signal them."

"No need. They've seen us. They're coming about."

"Okay." Tom sat back down. For a moment he watched the hull of the approaching craft. It was catching the light from the east, gleaming like a pearl on the dark waters. He heard in memory his own voice say to Victor, *he brought down their Lynx to make sure.* It was stupid, really. In the whole of this night, not once had Tom thought beyond that one end of Tremaine's. To disable the chopper and escape with his life…

And then what? Cast himself into a heaving waste of sea, lose himself beyond all hope of collecting his reward? What had he done the time before?

Arranged for his pickup, obviously. Tom frowned into the rapidly diminishing distance between the launch and the raft. Now she was close enough to pick out her lines. She was powerful and sleek, scudding across the grey-green swell. Someone's private vessel—yes, a Sunseeker. Very expensive.

Tom glanced at Vic, and saw him seeing it too. Completing the same thought. Their eyes met. Victor said softly, "If we needed to outrun that thing…"

"We couldn't. Could we?"

"No. And I'm sure there's no call to, but…have you still got my Browning?"

Tom started. It felt like a century ago that he had stood in the Porth Bay boathouse and taken Victor's service gun from him. He had tucked it into an inner pocket of his jacket. "Yeah, I do. I think Flynn's probably sleeping on it. Hang on a minute."

Flynn was curled on his side against the hull, a motionless, abandoned shape among the coats Tom had bundled round him. Tom ran a hand over his hair, murmured his name, but he didn't respond. Carefully Tom shifted him far enough to extract the revolver from his damp coat, then straightened back up into the daylight. Victor was waiting for him, one hand outstretched.

"What?" Tom asked him, smiling wryly. "You think I wouldn't use it, if… I'm as much a soldier as you are, Vic."

Victor nodded. "Probably more so. But you got paid to fix the bullet holes, Doc. I got paid to put them in."

Tom thought about it. The Sunseeker was only a couple of hundred yards out from them now. It jarred his instincts, to relinquish any possibility of guarding Flynn. But he knew that Vic would be the better shot, and after a moment he handed the weapon over. "Well, like you say. I'm sure there's no call. But…"

"If there is, I'll make 'em count." He tucked the Browning under the belt of his jeans, untucking his shirt to conceal it. "No sense in coming on all lairy if it's just a friendly passing millionaire, now, is there?"

It was not. The launch accelerated violently on its approach, then at the last moment cut its engines, slewing silently round the raft's stern. Tom was reminded of a cat's final circling move in pursuit of its prey, to cut off an exit route, to display itself and its powers for the sheer joy of it. He saw Vic's move for the gun— saw him abort it, as he understood, in the growing dawn light, that the two men at the rail were holding enough firepower in their hands to cut him and Tom in half in one burst of semiautomatic fire.

The men were strangers. Whoever they had expected to find on the downed helicopter's raft, it was probably not the village doctor and a boatbuilder. That, and the deep sleep he'd just seen Flynn at last surrendered to, barely visible under the raft's canopy, gave Tom cause to hope. *We just came out to help. No, we didn't find anyone.*

Then the launch drifted to a halt. Through the wheelhouse glass, Tom saw a low ray of sunlight catch on red hair. A strapping six-foot Bronze Age Celt unfolded himself from the pilot's seat and came to stand at the rail between his colleagues. "Well, freeze my piss if it's not Dr. Tom," Rob Tremaine boomed, grinning broadly. "My personal bad bloody penny. I have no idea what the fuck you're doing out here, but I'm willing to bet you've got something I want." And Tom heard a rustling of fabric from the canopy behind him, and a small, gut-punched moan as Flynn staggered out and dropped to his knees on the raft's deck behind him, and all hope died.

Rob Tremaine surveyed them. He didn't seem the worse for his ditch into the sea. His expression was genial, and although his hair was still damp, he had on a fresh white shirt. Aside from his two flanking gunmen, he looked like a wealthy yacht captain about to extend the hospitality of his boat. His gaze fastened on Flynn. "Ah, there you are," he said pleasantly. "Nice run, Flynnie. Nice try. But now come here."

Tom supposed that, to Flynn, it was like a corpse sitting up on its slab—like a fresh grave mound stirring and vomiting back its dead. He was too far away from Flynn to extend a hand, to do more than whisper his name as he struggled upright. "Flynn. No..."

Flynn glanced at him. Tom could see no light in his eyes. His blue-tinged lips parted as if he was about to speak, but then he turned away—allowed one of Tremaine's fellow smugglers to reach over and half-lift, half-haul him off the raft and across the rail onto the Sunseeker.

He stood in front of Tremaine. His back was straight, his hands by his sides. Tremaine examined him bleakly for a few moments. Flynn remained passive under the inspection, looking at the deck. Then Tremaine, without a shift of his vulpine mask, drew back a hand and cuffed him so hard round the side of the head that Flynn dropped like a stone.

Tom hauled a helpless breath. "Flynn!" he yelled. "Christ, Tremaine, stop!"

Tremaine raised his head. Tom realised what had set the gleam of satisfaction in his eyes—the raw panic in his own voice. It would do Flynn no good to show his captor the depth of their bond now, and he shut himself up, muscles setting fiercely. Flynn had pushed up off the deck, but only as far as his knees. His head was down. Once he was sure he could do it, Tom said his name again—again, over and over, but only calmly. A lifeline, an invisible touch extended to him across the water.

Flynn blinked and seemed to shudder back to life. He raised his head. When he spoke, he sounded pretty calm too. "It's okay, Tom. Please don't get yourself killed over this. Over me. I'll be okay."

No, not calm. Resigned, as if fate had extended its fist from the ocean and seized him. Tom lurched forward. The gunman at the rail snapped up his rifle, and he felt Vic's restraining hand at the back of his shirt. "Flynn…"

"Oh, he's right," Tremaine said, dropping one big hand down onto the crown of Flynn's head, his fingers entangling brutally tight in his hair. "He's actually not worth you dying for. I had you checked out, you know, Dr. Tom, when I saw how Flynnie was looking at you. You're a good man. Decorated three times for pulling injured soldiers off the battlefield. I bet you never told this worthless little piece of shit about that."

Flynn shivered. He fixed Tom with a look of pure love. "No," he said faintly. "He didn't."

"So despite the massive inconvenience you've caused me— and yourself, because if you hadn't seen me in the Penzance casualty, I'd never have had to take out an expensive and apparently nonrefundable hit on you—you're getting a second chance, Tom." He gave Flynn's hair one brutal twist, then reached down to his collar and jerked him upright. "Go home." He shook his head, and Tom saw a sadness gather on his harsh-boned face. Tom could have pitied him, in another world. "I don't know. Maybe I've learned to value men. Two years ago, I came back for Flynn because I loved him. This time he's just my hostage."

He nodded to one of his companions, who ducked inside the cabin and started the Sunseeker's engines. The second man remained where he was, semiautomatic trained on the raft. The larger vessel began to move, setting up a ripple in the water, a deep throbbing vibe in the air. Peripherally, Tom saw Flynn begin to struggle, and knew that he should watch—that it was his last chance to see, before Rob Tremaine pinched out all the light and the heat that had returned to his world.

But Tom looked at Victor instead. They both were soldiers. It was one glance—bright, vital, electric. *Not your fight, Vic, but...* Victor nodded minutely. The launch drew alongside, her pilot beginning his manoeuvre away. There was a moment.

Victor used the raft's gunwale tube as a springboard and grabbed the rail of the launch. He was not fast, but the sight of him in sudden, unlikely motion was impressive, twelve stone of British ex-military on the move, purposeful, heedless of consequence. It startled Tremaine's gunman so much that he could not snap the rifle's safety off before Vic was on top of him, shoving the gun muzzle up. Vic felled him with a sledgehammer punch that sent him and the rifle straight over the rail into the water. Then he turned—it was the last possible second, the boats moving apart—and grabbed Tom's outstretched hands, hauling him onto the launch.

Tom made a bad scramble of it. He lurched over the top of the rail and hit the Sunseeker's deck with a thud that knocked the breath from him. He was running on love and adrenaline, and almost empty. The only advantage of his uncontrolled leap was the place where it ended—at Rob Tremaine's feet, causing him to start back with a muffled curse. To loosen, for an instant, his grip on Flynn, who didn't need a second invitation.

On his feet again, clinging to the rail, Tom watched matters conclude themselves. The Sunseeker's pilot, slowly coming up to speed, had snapped off the engine and exited the wheelhouse, rifle in hand, but too late. Vic, planted casually in her prow, had the Browning cocked and ready in an easy two-handed grip, covering her whole deck. "Drop it," he advised, and the pilot obeyed, then followed Vic's gestured order that he should kick the weapon over to Tom.

Tom reached down for it blindly. He could not look away from the scene unfolding in the stern. Flynn, who five minutes before had been sleeping like a displaced angel on the raft, was straddled over Rob Tremaine, whom he had felled with an elbow to the gut and a haymaker as soon as Tremaine was off balance. His face was blank as a mountain lion's, and he was in the process of beating his captor unconscious.

A time and a place for everything. Tom knew that a few seconds of this would benefit Flynn more than years of psychiatry, and he stayed back, letting his lover get a few more good ones in. He could hear his own shocked laughter and drew deep breaths to contain it, to stop his head from spinning and keep himself on his feet for the time it would take to end this. Only when blood flew in a spray from Tremaine's nose did he step forward. He put a hand on Flynn's shoulder. "Flynn, love. Flynn! That'll do. It's over."

Flynn jerked round. For a moment his eyes betrayed no recognition, and Tom went cold. Then he blinked, and ran a hand across his brow. "Tom?"

"Yeah. Come on. Come on, stand up. Let him go." Tom put a hand into his armpit and helped lever him upright, away from

Tremaine, who lay coughing and spitting out blood on the deck. "Vic's got him covered. Okay?"

"Okay, but…"

"Bastard!" It was a broken-voiced explosion, a curse and a sob all at once. Tremaine, shoving up onto one elbow, dragged his hand over his mouth. "I did love you," he rasped. "I'd have done anything. I *gave* you everything. And then some hard-luck story with a dog and a drink problem came along, and…that was it. You were gone. I've lost you."

"Love?" Flynn repeated incredulously. Tom tightened his grip on him and felt Flynn's hand come blindly to cover his own. "You're fucking kidding, aren't you? You *lost* me two years ago, Rob. I just didn't remember till now."

Rob's face twisted. "Then fuck you, you thankless little… Christ, do you think you can be happy with him? You'll never run with the angels, you nutcase. What'll he do for your nightmares? When… When you start begging to be hurt?"

Tom put a restraining hand on Flynn's chest. But to his surprise, when Flynn turned to him, his face was calm. The terrible sea-green fury had evaporated from his eyes. He said softly, "It's all right, love. Let me go for a second."

Tom obeyed, falling back against the rail. He was absolutely, terminally exhausted, but he thought that it was over now. That he could lower his guard. Suddenly the rifle in his hand weighed a ton, and he cracked on its safety and let it down onto the deck. He watched while Flynn went to crouch by Rob Tremaine, staring into his face. "Rob. *You* were my nightmare, you arsehole. You were the only hurt. You don't know what love is, and…nor did I, until a couple of weeks ago." He glanced up at Tom, tired face softening. "I'm all right, Tom. Just gonna go find some rope to tie up this sucker. And hopefully some gaffer tape for his mouth."

Tom felt a grin starting, in spite of the dizzying spin the world was beginning around him. He stood, clutching the rail, while Flynn went aft. He was vaguely aware of Victor, on his other side, hauling off the Sunseeker's pilot into her wheelhouse. *Over*, he thought. *All over. Nothing's gonna spoil if I drop now.*

On the deck, Rob Tremaine groaned. Tom watched detachedly. He probably was in a lot of pain. Well, couldn't happen to a nicer man. Victor was shouting to Flynn from the cabin, indicating that he'd found a length of cable twine and had some to spare after tying up his own man. There was a massive grin in Victor's voice, as if he hadn't enjoyed himself so much in ages. Tom supposed all kinds of demons had been cast overboard on this long night.

Tremaine convulsed. His head jerked back, banging off the deck. His groan pitched into a raw yell of agony—and Tom, who was tired, stupid, and a healer by instinct as well as by trade, shoved off the rail and went to kneel beside him.

Tremaine had a snub-nosed pistol holstered up in a harness at his back. *Of course he has*, Tom thought, sitting up with the muzzle of it buried in his chest. His seizure had allowed him to reach round under his oilskin and grab it. *He wasn't gonna be the west coast's first unarmed bloody arms dealer, was he?* Distantly he heard Flynn's cry. He was in the doorway to the wheelhouse—frozen, his face a blank. Behind him, Tom could see Victor glancing up, turning too slowly. Both too far away, too slow, to help.

Tom found that he didn't mind. All that bothered him was his own utter stupidity in losing this game for them both, after all that they had done. So much passion and courage, and he had screwed it all on the last roll of the dice. He said harshly, "I'm sorry, Flynn."

Flynn did not move. "Okay," he whispered. "Okay, love. Just stay still."

Tremaine had coiled up with horrible virility. He sat on the deck, regarding Tom calmly. His eyes were utterly cold. Tom knew that there was no possibility of bluff, no chance that this was an empty threat. That he was probably counting down the last seconds of his life. He thought of everything he ought to say to Flynn, and realised he wasn't about to reveal one word of it to this monster. He prayed—he believed—that Flynn knew. He closed his eyes.

"Robert."

Christ, that voice would melt stone. Tom's eyes flew open. He saw Tremaine helplessly glance towards it too, breaking their deadlock. Flynn was emerging—slowly, slowly—from the cabin. His hands were up, palms out. The morning light, brilliant now, painted him in bronze and gold. His movements were quiet, serene. He took one step out from the wheelhouse and onto the desk, and Tremaine didn't move. "Rob," he said. "Okay. Okay, what would it take?"

Tremaine frowned. Tom, drawing one careful breath after another, wondered if he, too, were utterly distracted by the sight of Flynn—salt-rimed and weary, but somehow blazing out a charm Tom had never seen turned up to full and now could not tear his gaze from. "What… What would what take?"

"For you to let Tom go. Come on, Robbie, darlin'. You're right, okay?" One more step, a cat deciding where to plant its next pad. Tom's throat dried out, but the pressure of the gun muzzle at his chest didn't alter. "You're right. I've been a thankless little shit, haven't I? But Tom's not what you want. You *know* what you want, and I'm right here."

A silence extended itself. Tom listened to it carefully. All his life he had loved the music of this world—had grown up with it interwoven with his thoughts, the rhythms of his day. Wind song, lifting from the south as the sun touched the water. The soft slap of waves on a harbour wall or hull. And always, like bright silver stitches in the tapestry, seagull cries, lifting up the sky from the earth, creating wild free space for thought to take flight. He found it hard to believe that he had ever chosen to exchange it for the clatter of desert gunfire. He would have liked to hear it for many years more. For a lifetime, with Flynn…

Too late for everything now. But he would not let Robert take him. Wouldn't be his price. Flynn was still approaching, one gentle step at a time. Bracing, Tom got ready to make the move that would force Tremaine's hand—by which he would transform himself from hostage to worthless vacant flesh. He raised his head and met Flynn's eyes. "Flynn, stay away from him."

Flynn ignored him. He came and crouched down a yard or so from Tremaine, just out of arm's reach. He said quietly, "Are you gonna let him go, Rob?"

Tremaine swallowed, the sound of it a gravelly scrape. "What—for you?" he choked out. "I told you already, sweetheart. Your gold plate's worn off. I know you now."

Smiling, Flynn shrugged. "Well, I know you too, don't I? Come on. You don't care if I'm solid. Let's put Tom and Vic back on the raft—your mates too—and take this boat and go. We can have the life you want."

Oh God. It was going to work. Tom saw, through a veil of nightmare, that something in Robert Tremaine was lost enough, damaged enough, to reach out for the broken-glass future Flynn was offering. To his astonishment, he heard the ratchet of the safety going on. He felt a diminution of the pistol's pressure at his chest, then a cessation, leaving a numb patch behind it.

Flynn's hand was out. Tremaine eased back a little way on his haunches. His free hand began its journey to meet Flynn's, a brutal, meaty shape that eclipsed the morning sun. For a moment Tom saw him, vision knocked back by shock to a child's unprejudiced simplicity, as the monster from the deeps—the undying beast of closet and bedroom shadows. Flynn would vanish whole into his maw. Tom hauled a breath, whispered, to God and the wild clear sky, *no!*—and lunged to dive between them.

Tremaine's eyes snapped to frozen steel. For an instant, Tom had an impression of looking at the tips of a pair of ice picks. The pistol made the first sound of its safety-catch release, muzzle swinging back towards Tom's heart. Flynn yelled, "Robert!"— gave Tremaine one instant to look up, to understand—unshipped Victor's service Browning from his belt, and shot Tremaine squarely between the eyes.

Vic stumbled out of the cabin. He was sheet white. Tom saw Flynn nod at him and hold out the Browning towards him in a trembling fist. He said, "Ta, Victor. Nice pass," and dropped to his knees on the deck.

Chapter Ten
Harbour

Two helicopters descended on their shocked little scene barely ten minutes after its ending, one to commandeer the traffickers and their boat, the other to airlift survivors. Victor declined the ride—a sailor to the end, he couldn't bear the abandonment even of the ASaC raft—and volunteered to sail her home.

Tom did not want to be airlifted, not as a patient. He was fine. He did not want to let Flynn out of his sight, even as far as the cockpit of the Devon chopper that had come to their rescue, not if he himself was going to be dragged off to the cabin and mollycoddled by large, determined military airmen. Flynn had calmly hailed their leader and requested radio access to begin his report, but he was grey with shock, going through the motions. Tom did not want to be admitted to the Hawke hospital wing on their arrival—he was a civilian, and, as he had already explained to the ASaC crew, he was fine.

Further, Tom disagreed passionately with Flynn's commanding officer's idea that an immediate debriefing was necessary. It would wait a few bloody hours, wouldn't it? While Tom was shouting about his own rights and Flynn's, and

Commander Hughes looking on in bemusement at being confronted like this on his own airbase—by the mild-mannered, reclusive village doctor from Sankerris, at that—Flynn briefly disappeared. Came back, and when Hughes left the room to take a phone call, laid a hand to Tom's arm. "Come with me."

The Mazda was parked outside a loading bay, whose open doors, and the chaos of an early-morning delivery coming through them, provided a neat exit. The guard on the west gate gave Flynn a conspiratorial smile and waved them through. Flynn took them home.

***

They were on the run, Tom supposed. The watchtower was bitterly cold, dank air catching in his lungs as Flynn pushed open the door. He had never really registered how cold the place could get, but he seemed to be feeling everything now, and gasped and shivered as Flynn led him into the living room. Flynn stood for a minute, distractedly propping him, rubbing warmth into his shoulders and arms. "Hang on a bit, love," he said. "I saw a scorch mark on the outside wall the other day. There's got to be an old chimney flue. Sit down while I work out where it is."

There, behind a panel Tom had never noticed. It was only lightly screwed into place—Flynn's first good tug pulled it back, revealing a hearth which, although filled with soot and the remains of jackdaws' nests, looked functional. Tom supposed he might have assumed the building had one somewhere, from the supply of neatly stacked firewood in a shed out the back, but it hadn't occurred. Flynn brought in armfuls of it. He rumpled up sheets of newspapers and set a flame beneath these and the jackdaws' twigs, watching carefully for signs that the chimney was blocked. When the kindling took and began cleanly to draw, he built the new blaze up with a few logs, got up and went to switch the heating on for water. To boil a kettle for tea.

***

Firelight on curving walls. Tom could not get used to it, to the shadow-dance cavern it made of his front room. Flynn had tried to persuade him to bed, or at least to the sofa, but he could not draw away from it yet. He sat curled up on the rug, looking into the flames. Flynn, who hadn't stopped since their arrival, continued his anxious pacing back and forth in search of domestic comforts.

On his next pass, Tom grabbed his wrist. "Flynn."

"Yes. You all right? I'm just gonna go—"

"You had to kill him. God, love. I'm so sorry."

Flynn's legs buckled. He fell to his knees on the flagstones. For a moment, he looked bitterly angry, and Tom could see that he had pulled him down mid-flight. "Don't," he said hoarsely. "I've already mourned him, as far as he was worth it."

"I know. That's different from having to shoot him."

"A technicality. Victor would've done it, if he'd had an angle. He just slipped me the gun." Flynn shook his head, smiling weakly at the memory. "A cool hand, your Vic."

"Yeah. Yeah, he is." Tom reached up. "I've had two good mates tonight, haven't I? Come here, love."

Tom laid him gently out on the rug. He was still wearing his flight suit, for God's sake. Neither of them had noticed, as if it had become a part of him. It had dried on him in places, but his chest and stomach, as Tom unzipped it, ran a hand up under the T-shirt beneath, were clammy cold.

"Get you out of this," he murmured, and between them, awkwardly, they removed the heavy garment, with its straps, radio, integral torch, signalling gear. The sight of the navy-issue thermal leggings thus revealed cracked them both to laughter, then Flynn raised a hand to cover his eyes.

Tom held him. He warmed him as best he could with his body, lay over him and shielded him. It was a long time before Flynn could speak, and when he did, his voice was a faint rasp. "I want to tell you I loved him. But I didn't. Not ever. Not even at the beginning, before he…"

"Doesn't make it any easier, for you to do what you did."

"No. But what was I doing with him? Why did I stay?"

Tom knew that these questions, though urgent, were not ones he was meant to answer. They were things for Flynn to work out over time. Easing back far enough to see him, he smiled, and Flynn seemed to find that enough of an answer for now—put a hand round the back of Tom's neck and drew him down. "Oh, Tom. Make me forget him."

Can't do that either, not for long. But maybe for a while. Kissing him, Tom obeyed the guiding grip on his wrist. He slid a hand into the awful thermal underwear, which didn't seem to be doing him much good—he was even cold there, and he remained soft beneath Tom's caress. Hardly surprising…

Tom ignored his moan of distress and embarrassment, got stiffly to his feet and went to fetch the blanket from the sofa. "Come on, you. Get those hideous pants off and wrap yourself in this. And sit down in the armchair."

"No. I'm okay. I'll get there in a minute. Don't stop what you were doing."

"Not about to. Just don't think I can suck you off from ground level tonight."

Flynn looked at him, wide-eyed. Then he took Tom's hand and scrambled upright. "Christ almighty," he whispered. "What is it about hearing you talk like that, my nice-mannered doctor?"

"Did the trick, did it?" Tom helped him strip out of the rest of his clothes, then gently pressed him down into the chair. He knelt between his thighs.

"Oh. See for yourself."

Tom drew a breath of admiration. He passed the blanket blindly up to him, unable to take his eyes off his cock, which had lifted in sudden splendour and was still filling now, casting rose-gold shadows in the firelight.

"What brought that on?" he whispered, flickering him one dark-eyed, teasing glance. "Just me saying that I want to suck you off? Just..." He paused long enough to push his hands up the back of Flynn's thighs, grasping tight when he gasped and arched to make room. "Hearing that I want you to shove that down my throat, all the way down?"

"Oh, *Tom*..."

Tom nodded in satisfaction. Flynn was hard to his belly now, his hands clenched white-knuckle tight on the arms of the chair. "I see. Good lad. Mind you don't pull out when you come, either. I want you."

"Tom... God, you sadistic bastard, have pity."

Tom glanced up. There was laughter in the plea, and real anguish. He had wrapped a warm restrictive grip around the base of Flynn's cock, and each time the convulsions of orgasm began in him, the short hard thrusts that would end it, he closed the circle of his finger and thumb and squeezed, driving the impulse hotly back inside him, never ceasing the movement of lips and tongue up and down his shaft, across the head. Flynn was ready, skin warm under his free hand, the last of the sea-chill driven out from him. Tom stroked his hip by way of response, and continued, rhythmic, merciless.

"Oh. Too good, lover, too sweet. You can't make me last forever." A racked, unbreathing pause, in which Tom almost heard Flynn's memories surfacing through the ice of shock. "He never did this to me. Never went down on me. God, why? He used to make me, like it was his royal bloody due. Ah, Tom, let me come!"

Tom heard the desperate sincerity in it and relented, releasing his hold as the next peak hit. His breadth of experience was no more than average, and he was out of practice. It took an effort of will to allow Flynn to thrust the last couple of inches into his mouth, to relax enough to take him. Breathing was out of the question—the head of his cock had slipped over the root of his tongue and into his airway.

Flynn moaned, a sound of absolute urgency and need, and Tom's fright, the edge of panic, burned off in exhilaration. *Yes. I can set you free.* He grabbed Flynn's backside in both hands, dragged him up and forward even as he struggled back in a last-ditch effort of self-control. Tom tasted blood and salt—wondered, for one flashing instant, if Flynn shared his terrible vision of Rob Tremaine's white face, blank with surprise, the neat black hole punched in his brow—then the wave hit, wiping his mind clear of anything but the moment and of Flynn, bursting deep in his throat, crying out, head arching wildly back, bracing on his arms. Coughing and laughing, he hung on to him for dear life.

"Oh my God. Tom. Are you all right?"

Slowly Tom got his head up. He wiped his mouth with his hand and beamed exhaustedly up at Flynn. "Fine. You?"

"Do you have to ask?" Flynn leaned and kissed him, sending a hot shiver through Tom at the thought of how he must be tasting his own come. He tried not to let him feel the locked-iron effort it was taking him to stay still, but Flynn's touch became listening, attentive. "You're not fine. What have I been doing to you?"

"Nothing I didn't wholly and joyously ask for." Tom ran an unsteady hand through his hair. "But I admit, sweetheart…I'm about done for tonight."

Flynn glanced down. The fire was burning brightly now, throwing sharp shadows. Tom's jeans were still slightly damp too, and clinging to him. Flynn said softly, "Not quite."

"Oh, that. Just help me up to bed, or…dump me here by this nice fire. Ignore it. It'll go away."

Flynn extended gentle fingertips. He ran an exploratory, moth-like touch over Tom's face. "I think we can do better for you than that."

He went upstairs. Tom, laid out on sofa cushions by the fire where Flynn had put him, took in the beautiful naked sight of him padding up the spiral staircase, too worn out to be other than mildly curious as to his purposes. He was aching with unsatisfied desire, but really didn't think there was much hope for him. Would be happy, he thought, if Flynn would only come and stretch out and sleep here beside him.

Happy? He'd be fucking ecstatic. Watching him come back down the tower's spiral, he said, "I thought I'd lost you. When Vic told me you'd gone out with Rob… I thought I'd lost you."

"You found me." Flynn knelt beside him. He opened his palm and let Tom see the tube of lubricant he'd gone up to find. There were tears in his eyes again. Smiling unsteadily, he cast a glance back towards the stairs. "We started something up there. You and me. And we didn't finish it, because of Rob."

"Flynn, wait. You don't have to…"

"Hush." Flynn reached out and pressed the pads of his fingers to Tom's lips. He moved to straddle him, clumsily undoing the buttons of his jeans with his free hand. "It's all right. I'm better now. Unless he forced me, I never let him touch me again, you know, after we… Not like that."

"He must've been delighted," Tom said hoarsely.

"Yeah. He was a real gent about it. But I'm fine." He uncapped the lubricant, seized avid hold of Tom's shaft as it rose. "I know how tired you are, love. You don't have to do a thing."

He moved with cautious passion, bearing his weight on his thighs. Tom knew a moment's uncertainty, a fear that he would not be able to manage, or would not know how, but Flynn reached round behind himself and placed a guiding grip on his cock. This time his face betrayed no pain as Tom slipped inside, only a hunger that increased with every inch of his progress, deeper and deeper until Tom knew he was at full engagement, stretching him to his limits.

"Flynn," he whispered, trying to thrust up.

"No. Lie still, lie still, let me…" He shifted himself up a little, then back down, breathing shallowly, never for one instant taking his eyes off Tom's. After a few more repeats of this shy, hampered movement, his control faltered, and he jerked forward, shuddering, trying not to lose balance. "Tom… Sorry."

"Come on." Tom seized his wrists, showing him where he could rest his hands without hurting. "Let me have you."

"I thought I'd lost you too. When I came out on deck, and there he was with a gun on you… It was like time stopped for me, and his went on. He was gonna shoot you."

"You stopped him. It's over."

Flynn groaned and arched his spine. Tom was in him to the root, so deep that he could feel the warm squeeze of his balls when Flynn pressed down. Nowhere further to go. Flynn's smallest shift sent lightning bolts of pleasure through him. Despite having come so long and hard down Tom's throat not half an hour before, his cock leapt.

The sight of it tore Tom apart. He reached and seized Flynn's shoulders, crying out his name, writhing up unstoppably to find him, to meet him, stroke for stroke, passion for passion. The shocks of pain that went through him at each thrust bonded themselves to his pleasure till the two were inextricably entwined and he was coming, yelling in triumph and anguish as Flynn convulsed to orgasm around him.

***

The first thing Tom saw, by late-morning light pouring through the tower's east window, was the blue-green crest of a wave. He lay for a long time, watching the elegant shape through the net of his eyelashes. He was still half-asleep. The fire had died down to its ashes, but these glowed a bright, extraordinary pink in the sunlight, radiating heat into the room. He had been made comfortable on the sofa cushions, the blanket tucked around him, a pillow pushed under his head. When finally he understood what he was looking at, he broke into a broad smile.

"Morning, handsome."

The other pleasure tugging at his mind had been the scent of fresh-made coffee. He sat up as Flynn crouched beside him, or tried to. "Ow. Christ."

Quickly Flynn set the two mugs down on the hearthside and took hold of his shoulders. "Yeah. Anyone would think you'd been in a car crash. Take it easy."

"I will. I thought that had gone back to the Marazion studio."

"Well, not quite. It got as far as the boot of my Mazda, and then I just drove it around. Suppose I was hoping I might get another chance to ambush you with it."

Tom shifted, got enough balance to take hold of the mug Flynn passed him. Not all his aches and pains were bad. On reflection, he felt thoroughly, expertly ambushed. "Well, it's bloody beautiful."

"Can it stay this time?"

"Yes. Can you?"

Flynn knelt in front of him. For a moment Tom wondered if, even now, he had said too much. Flynn had endured for two years the worst griefs and humiliations one man could inflict on another. Perhaps it would take him longer than this, to learn how to deal with kindness. With love, because that was what was going on here, what had been going on since they had struggled together out of the Porth Bay surf. Perhaps it would take him forever.

Flynn said unsteadily, "I've got to go to Hawke to debrief. Mike Findlay's coming out here to check you over, and do whatever one doctor does to another for absconding from his ICU, I should think."

He paused. Tom gazed at him. His presence seemed to him as fragile and unlikely as that of the sea-glass wave. Then Flynn leaned in and kissed him. "Then I'll come home, and…I'll pick up your dog on my way."

***

The first real gale of winter, and Belle would not hush up. Tom had never known her to behave like this. He and Flynn watched her prowling the bounds of the living room and kitchen, raising her eerie, seldom-heard bark every few strides. "Belle, what's got into you?"

"Do you think she's ill?"

"Maybe." Tom called the dog over, and the two of them checked her from nose to tail, looking for swollen gums, injured paws, a tender belly. She submitted patiently to the examination, then moved gently but inexorably away from them and resumed her prowl.

Maybe it was the weather, though Tom had never known her disturbed by the wildest of storm nights before. It wasn't good timing. He and Flynn both had an early start the next morning, and the early night they had promised themselves had turned into a bruising, happy, hours-long struggle round the tower's upper room. An early start and a new job, for Flynn, who after the investigation into Rob Tremaine's death had received a startlingly thorough military apology and reinstatement to the Maritime Security squad. He had been offered his old berth at Portsmouth, but had turned it down. Cornwall was his home now. Cornwall and Tom. The watchtower too, although both of them had begun tentatively to discuss moving out, to a place not under a demolition order, which did not run with damp from October to May and cost so much to heat they would toss coins for the privilege of not opening the bill.

Tom's exile was over. He did not need his fortress anymore, but anxiety would still touch him at the prospect of the move, for reasons he could not define. The habit of defence, he supposed. Flynn, who knew by now his every fear, was in no hurry. Told him, between kisses, that he would live with him forever in his world's-edge ruin.

Belle kept on barking. Aware that Flynn was watching him in tired amusement, Tom sat her down in front of him and talked to her as he would to an intelligent teenager, patiently explaining that, since everything was all right, and he and Flynn needed their sleep, she should really settle down now. It shouldn't have worked, but the poor dog listened to him with every appearance of comprehension, and when he was finished, went and lay down in her bed in the kitchen, tail tucked, ears clamped tight to her skull.

Tom shrugged, holding out a hand to Flynn. "God knows. Come on, love. Big day for you tomorrow. Today, actually, in about five hours' time."

"Tom, would you think I was off my head if I didn't take it?"

"What—the reinstatement?"

"Yeah. I loved it, but…I love the rescue work too. Better, I think."

Tom smiled. It hadn't been his place to talk to Flynn about it, and he had wanted to see him fully compensated by the service which had been so quick to send him down, but… "Whatever you want," he said, and Flynn came to him, as if he was fire in the darkness, sunshine in winter's heart. "You're a good lad, Flynn."

And this wouldn't get them to bed any sooner, either, or at least not there to sleep. Carefully, deliberately, he disentangled them, pushed him in the direction of the stairs.

***

Quarter to four in the morning. Tom registered the time at the same instant as a warm, wet press against his ear, and rolled onto his side, moaning. "Flynn, love… What the fuck?"

Something by the bed. Tom jolted upright in visceral panic, limbic brain seeing only the wolf in the fold, a beast with glowing eyes. It took him a moment to recognise Belle, who was too well-mannered ever to invade his room uninvited, and never came up during the night. He felt Flynn's waking movement at his side, and he sat, gazing out at the red-tinged waning moon, at its eerie light reflected in Belle's pupils. Her silence was eloquent.

"Flynn," he said, after a few seconds. "There's something not right."

"Other than the fact that you mistook your bloody dog for me?" Flynn enquired politely, making him snort with laughter but then put out a hand to Flynn's arm, immobilising him, listening.

"I'm serious. Something…"

A tremor struck the tower. The hairline crack on the far wall, which over the past month had expanded unnoticed to a rift an inch wide, gaped suddenly huge, in a gunfire-roar of falling masonry. The floor lurched.

Tom leapt out of bed. He grabbed Flynn, grabbed his dog and shoved them ahead of him down the tower's spiral stairs. He tore open the great wooden door, which in these days of healing was not always locked, any more than the dishes were always done or the bed linen ironed. He pushed Flynn out into the night, barefoot out onto the wet turf, and together they ran in Belle's wildly barking wake until they stumbled and fell in a tangle, catching at each other, scrambling a desperate few yards farther from the cliff's crumbling edge.

The tower went down in majesty. Her seaward side had collapsed, but she held her ghostly moonlit form for five more seconds, while the cliff top avalanched away, cutting her foundations from beneath her. Then, with a thunderous howl, she was gone.

Flynn and Tom clung together on the turf. Belle, having made her point, transformed to her mute self and calmly came to sit beside them. Tom could not get breath into his lungs—or, when he could, it exited straight away in drowning gasps that suddenly for some reason began to break into laughter. "Oh…*fuck*," he managed eventually. "Flynn… God, Flynn, I love you!" And Flynn, who over the last months had said it to him, affectionately and often, never seeming to expect reply, turned to him in wonder.

Epilogue

Tom walked on the edge of the sea, which had restored the world to him. He was working full-time in the Penzance casualty department now, and had less opportunity to wander the lonely Porth beach with Belle, but the journey home was shorter, only ten minutes or so, in the replacement Land Rover he had bought when his insurance company finally decided he had not flipped his last one off the road on purpose and paid up.

Wrestling a slimy stick from Belle's jaws so that he could throw it again, Tom cast an amused look up to the car park where the vehicle was parked. She was similar in all respects to the last, except that, to Flynn's bewilderment, he had chosen an older model still. Well, where was the point in knocking the crap out of new models on these roads, he had explained to him, and he had spent the rest of the payout on a custom-built rack for the Mazda to carry Flynn's surfboard.

Ten minutes home, to the house on the beachfront he shared with Flynn. Neither of them had lost their taste for world's-edge living, but this one was built on firm foundations, and although it stood in stern isolation near the dunes, was within sight and a short drive of friends. Of Victor Travers, whose business was once again Porth's main employer but did not keep Vic from his duties as volunteer helmsman on the lifeboat; of Florrie's frequent dinner invitations, to which Chris Poldue and Gavin Wilkes would turn up too, shy and formal with each other even in this friendly company, but together at least.

Tom came to a halt on the sand. A familiar ragged-edged thump was beginning on the edge of the wind, more a vibration than a sound, disturbing his eardrums and the marrow of his bones. He looked up, instinctively reaching for Belle. He would never get used to it, he knew. Never be able to see the Hawke Lake SAR chopper sweeping seaward without a pain like ice in his heart. All the fears in Tom's life now were rational and quite real. Flynn, restored to himself, was a force of nature, a fire that burned so brightly Tom could scarcely look. No storm daunted him, no winter night so bitter that he would not haul himself reluctantly out of Tom's arms to answer the call.

No. The cliffs here were steep and had bounced back the sound of the rotors from their grey flanks—Flynn was coming home. The Sea King appeared on the horizon, and he braced up, grinning, waving wildly. It was Flynn's great joy in life to buzz him if he saw him on the beach, to swing the great roaring craft as low as he dared over his head. Tom set off at a run for the car park, Belle bounding in silent delight at his heels. The roar of the engines got into Tom's blood. He and Flynn would race to intercept one another, at a mission's end, to be the first one home, the one who got to tear open the door for the other's arrival and tackle him onto the sofa, the carpet, the stairs, sometimes even the bed if they could wait.

Great breakers crashed on the Porth Bay shore. The only non-living thing Tom would have salvaged from the watchtower was the sea-glass wave. Their home had its other treasures now, but by tacit agreement they had not replaced it—it was a phenomenon that had belonged to its time. All things were so, Tom knew, and he no longer tried to hold on. All things could fall and be lost: David's cairn, a handful of quartz in an avalanche, scattered, unforgotten. Flynn was the tide of Tom's life now, the wave that surrounded him, that surged beneath him bringing ecstasy, that delivered him safely to shore. On lifeboat nights, search-and-rescue nights, nights of storm, when he was off duty, Tom went to the harbourside RNLI station and helped Florence make tea, talked quietly to the others waiting there.

You made the best of every second you could spend with them, and then…you let them fly.

About the Author

Harper Fox is the author of many critically acclaimed M/M romance novels, including Stonewall Book Award-nominated *Scrap Metal* and *Brothers of the Wild North Sea*, a Publishers Weekly Best Book. To find out more about Harper and see updates on her current writing projects, please visit www.harperfox.net.